The Diaries

The End

James Purcell

ISBN:1503002071
ISBN-13:978-1503002074

CONTENTS

ACKNOWLEDGMENTS

I would just like to thank everyone on-line and off-line, from all over the world, who have given me their support to help get this book to the level that you deserve.
Thank you everyone.
Special thanks to my mum, Ann Lee, and everyone on the various websites and groups who have taken the time to find and point out all my typo's and spelling mistakes.
Thank you to everyone who has given me editing tips, and last but not least, thank you to the following three people who, without their questions, this book would have remained a pile of notes and short stories on my hard drive.
Shirley Jarvil, Tracy Holmes and Allen Berkovitz.

Chapter I
Prologue.

The shining silver disc shone brightly in the night sky giving off not only light, but for those who are sensitive to the planets ebb and flow, an energy that charged the area around those who could sense it. It didn't matter that he couldn't see the glowing orb through the thick bank of cloud above him, even with the downpour, his kind were naturally sensitive to its energy, and it is that energy that gives them their ability to transform. Tonight is All Hallow's Eve, or Samhain in the old Druid calendar, a night that the humans believed the dead were able to walk the earth. In some ways the old stories were true. When the moon was at it's fullest and giving off the most energy, doorways could indeed be opened, but these portals did not lead to the world of the dead. This world, and the world that he had travelled from are separated from each other by a sub-world of pure energy where, if you could control the wild raging eddies of energy, you could create your own private world isolated from anyone, or anything else, that claimed the sub-world as home. This sub-world had been given a name and for those who were able to pass through it, they often referred to it as "The Veil." During the great scourging, started by this worlds King Uther Pendragon and his son Arthur, during the fifth and sixth centuries the dark creatures like his kind, along with the Druids, were forced to flee this world via portals called "Veil Gates," into the next world where their kind were not feared.

A few days back he had arrived in this world and had yet to see the sky through the constant, accursed rain. The rain was falling in such a torrent that his fur covered form, he was using was already soaked through and he feared the overly strong stench of wet dog fur would give him away. A shiver, caused by the icy touch of water creeping through his fur and along his skin, caused him to shudder sending what fur that wasn't held down with the weight of water to stand up on end. For the third time in ten minutes he stood up stretched and gave a huge canine shake in an attempt to shed some of the accumulated excess weight. He froze as the night sky was momentarily illuminated by a flash of lightning that turned the night into day and filled the atmosphere with the smell of burnt air and added to the electrically charged sensation around him. A few moments later the lightning was followed with a long rumble of thunder, so deep that it could be felt vibrating through the structure of the building that he was now using to watch the scene below.

He was not here by his own choice, he was here on a mission that had been handed to him by the Clans eldest leader. He had been promised that one day he would become the alpha male and lead the Clan in a war that would consume both worlds, but he would need to find the one human who was destined to lead the joint Clans in the battle. His mission, here, on this night, would be the start of a long plan that would take nearly twenty years for the destined chosen one to rise to where he would be needed.

"Why him, if he was to lead, why did he have to come to this god forsaken world?" He thought to himself. He knew the elder wasn't telling him everything, he could sense it in the elders voice, but when challenged, all the elder would say was that his blood was the key to influencing the chosen one.

In the streets below from where he watched, illuminated by the amber glow of both building and street gas lamps, the theatre doors opened and people spilled into the rain-soaked streets. They must have enjoyed the show as both the old and young we're talking in excited tones as they fled through the rain for the cover of a building or for one of the many horse-drawn carriages lining the streets below. All were oblivious to the watcher on the roof. Those who had the forethought to bring umbrellas fought to put them up, blocking the view of him looking down. He was watching for one particular couple, that according to the local broadsheets had just got engaged. For him, the girl was of no interest, but the boy, from the description provided by the elder, would be the key to the future of the worlds.

Looking up and down the street for any sign of this worlds law enforcers, he made sure the scene was clear of anything that would obstruct his plan, turning to the buildings rear and gripping the edge of the wall with a clawed hand that crushed the brickwork, launched himself from the roof to land in the darkened alley below without making the smallest of sounds, contrary to what a creature of his size would normally make. He edged his way to the entrance and peeked around the building edge to make sure that they were coming his way. Watching them approaching without the slightest idea of what would happen to them, he smiled and stepped far enough into the ally that no one would be able to see him before he could act.

Chapter II
The Murder of my beloved Eleanor.

We left the theatre after having enjoyed a wonderful show, but that was not the sole reason that we were acting like giddy children. Tonight we were celebrating the receiving of permission to marry. A few days ago, after keeping our relationship a secret, I had finally built up the courage to approach Professor Isaac Theologian, my mentor, and father of my beloved Eleanor, to ask for his permission to become engaged and married to his beloved daughter. He was working in his study at the time when I had asked him, he had sat there in silence for ages watching me, not making any movement or sound, but giving me his most stern look. I made every effort to keep eye contact as he watched me, but the ticking of the clock on the mantle piece behind him kept drawing my attention. Eventually he got up from his desk, walked over to the small drinks table that had a bottle of scotch, poured out a glass then turned back to me. Slowly the corner of his mouth raised in a smile.

"I wondered how long it would take you to ask me." he said, as he sat back behind his desk. I can vividly remember asking how he knew. "The way that you two have been carrying on, when you thought no one was watching, was hard to miss." he had replied after giving me a few moments to pull myself back together. After giving me his consent, he had, as an engagement gift, made arrangements for us to see a show, followed by a meal in one of the many high society restaurants that were located close to the theatre. Unfortunately his work at the University would provide cause for him not to see the show himself, but he had made arrangements for us to meet up at the restaurant after the show.

I was so excited about how events were unfolding that it took me a few minutes to realise that Eleanor wasn't beside me. I turned around and realised that she was standing stock still by the entrance to an alley. As I approached I noticed a large hand on her arm that dragged her into the gloom. A shadow appeared in the entrance as lighting flashed and I had the sinking feeling that we were now in deep trouble. I looked up and down the road for a police officer, or anyone who could help, but before I could shout for help, I was interrupted by a deep growling voice.

"Get in here without raising any noise," the man holding Eleanor ordered. I cast a last look around and stepped into the gloom after them.

"What do you want from us?" I asked, my voice shaking with fear.

"You!" he said with a chuckle,"nothing, You are going to stand there and watch as I kill your beautiful fiancée."

"Why?" I asked.

The man stepped closer. Light from a passing horseless carriage entered the alley reflecting off his eyes and I froze. This was no man that stood in front of me, he had broad shoulders, but his head was low with two sharply pointed ears that stood out on a head with a long face filled with sharp teeth. In my studies I had come across descriptions of his kind and only one word escaped my lips, causing him to smile. "Lycanthrope."

"Ah, I see you recognise my kind then" he said with a malicious smile.

"Why are you doing this?" I asked.

He smiled at me, then licked the side of Eleanor's face, causing her to faint. "This girl of yours smells good enough to eat. I am feeling hungry, so I may just start on her." he said, as his wolfen lips pulled back showing more of his razor sharp teeth, saliva pooled along his gums before dripping out onto her shoulder.

"But why us?" I asked, trying to feel for something to use as a weapon.

His smile returned as his eyes narrowed on me, a glitter of amusement in them. He stood there silently watching me, as I slowly stepped backwards towards the building walls that lined the alley searching for something, anything, that I could use as a weapon, my fingers grasped at something cold and round and I hoped it would do. I lifted up the object and watched as his smiled increased.

"So, you actually want to fight me?" the Lycanthrope taunted.

I watched as one of its hairy, almost human like clawed hands wrapped around Eleanor's neck and lifted her until her toes barely reached the ground. It's other hand came around and extending one finger like appendage, tipped with a sharp claw, run down her face cutting her skin just enough to make a pearlescent, crimson line of blood appear.

"Let her go," I said in a shaky voice, while brandishing the length of metal bar like a sword fighter I had seen in a book.

"Do you think you can stop me with that?" the Lycanthrope asked, amusement all over it's face.

I tightened my grip on my weapon and edged forward.

"Are you sure you want to do that?" he asked, lifting Eleanor up higher so that even her toes were now clear of the cobbled ground.

"Put her down," I repeated.

He grinned at me as he ripped open her dress around the shoulder area. I watched in horror as he slowly licked her skin causing goose bumps to rise on her pale skin causing her to wake up, her eyes were filled with horror. I did not know what to do.

Her normally green eyes were black with fear. I couldn't get my body to move. As I watched, a calmness came over her and her eyes turned back to their green colour. "Are you just going to stand like a village idiot while he kills me, James?"

"What can I do, he's likely to kill both of us."

"What about your promise to my father?"

"Eleanor, please …"

"Excuse me, but do you mind having this conversation another time, I am on a tight schedule." the werewolf said, lifting her up enough to make her choke.

"I know what you are monster, and I know that there will not be another time." Eleanor retorted.

"Really, pray tell me, what am I?" the werewolf asked.

"You are a Lycanthrope!" she stated flatly.

"And how would a woman like you know that?"

"Like my father and my fiancée, I have studied your kind, and know what you are, and the likely outcome of this meeting."

"Please tell me, my dear, what is going to happen?"

Eleanor turned to me "Goodbye James, don't let this monster kill you and don't throw your life away, or let my father throw your lives away."

Spurred on by her goodbye, I pushed away any fear about what would happen to me and ran at the Lycanthrope swinging the pole. His arm swung out and hit me in the chest knocking the air out of me, and sending me flying across the alley to smash into a wall. With a clanging sound my weapon bounced away, there was a sickening crunch from my arm, along with a sharp pain that was echoed by an equally sharp pain in my chest that caused me to double over. My eyesight blurred and tears welled up in them as I fought to get breath back into my lungs. I could hear him laughing and the sound of Eleanor's muffled screams. I reached out a hand and managed to pull myself to my feet, feeling pain in other parts of my body. Time seemed to slow down as he lifted her even higher, opened his jaws exposing his lethal fangs, then closing them down on her shoulder. I felt frozen, my legs wouldn't respond, all I could do was stand there and watch as his teeth sank deep into her flesh causing more of her pearlescent crimson blood to spill down her chest. It started as a small trickle as its teeth punctured the skin, but as its bite increased, so did the flow until it was a solid thick red stream.

Through all of this Eleanor screamed, but as the blood flow increased, her cries were reduced to a whimper before finally dying out. Her once blue dress now ran scarlet with her blood and as the last of the colour drained from her face, her skin turned to a ghostly shade of white. The Lycanthrope's eyes were fixed on me the whole time and I watched in horror as the corners of his lips raised in an animal-istic smile. Still, I stood there frozen to the spot un-able to stop the atrocity happening in front of me. With a sickening, soggy ripping sound, the were-wolf ripped a chunk out of her flesh.

"Ah, such a superb taste, quite an exquisite spec-imen." it said letting her fall to the floor and into the puddle of her own blood that had pooled below her, licking its lips to clean away any blood that was trapped in its facial fur.

"What are you going to do now?" I asked, final-ly able to speak.

"Nothing, I have done what I came to do, so I will now bid you farewell." and with a bow he turned and left me alone with the body of my fi-ancée. I didn't see the monster leave, I didn't even care if it was going to kill me, I stumbled over to Eleanor's body and fell to my knees, landing in her pool of blood. Carefully lifting her head from the ground, I knelt there holding her to my chest. The world around me completely forgotten.

Before the werewolf left the alley he turned around and looked back towards the boy crying over his woman. "Too easy," he said to himself watching the damage he had wrought, he stayed there quietly for a few minutes and then spoke up. "Don't think this is the last time our paths will cross, we have a future together and I will make sure that you stick to it." He stayed a bit longer to see if the boy would look up and comment, but the boy just ignored him. He turned away and headed down another alley, walked through a doorway into a room that was lit by a single candle.

"Is it done, Ketsueki Kage?" a soldier asked, stepping from the shadow and into the light.

"It has been done as you requested." he replied as his form shrunk back to human form," not in reply to the soldiers question, but to the figure sitting in the shadows of the room, "the first steps in this plan of yours have been taken and I hope that it works as you predict." He moved over to a table and started putting on the pile of clothes he had stashed here before starting his watch.

"Good work Kage, it will soon be time for us to return to Albion, but I must ask, what did you do with the girl?" came a question from the shadows.

"I was feeling hungry, and she smelled so good," he said feigning guilt.

"So, you took a bite out of her!" The old Clan leader stated, getting up from his seat in the shadows.

Kage licked his lips and smiled, "oh, she had such a divine taste, the females of this world are so much nicer to taste then our own," he said as he pulled on his shoes and tied up the laces. After a few minutes of adjusting his clothes, he watched as the old man walked to the door.

"It is time for us to return," he said pulling out a pocket watch, "if you would do the honour." he asked of the soldier who walked up behind him. The soldier nodded and walked out into the rain, a fog stirred around him, Kage, and the elder joined him, and when the fog had cleared, all three had disappeared.

Chapter III
The Restaurant.

"Another glass, sir?" the waiter asked, holding the bottle of red wine out to Isaac.

Isaac closed his pocket watch and looked down at the empty glass on the table in front of him. He was so intent in looking out the windows at the passers-by that he had forgotten he had even drunk from the glass. It was unlike Eleanor and James to be late for an appointment and he was starting to worry. From his table near the window he could see up and down the road, as well as all area's in the restaurant. He looked towards the door in case he had missed them walking past and checked his pocket watch for the umpteenth time. According to the theatre's timetable, twenty minutes had now past since the show had finished and they should already be here. A disturbance in the street caused him to look out the window. A couple on the other side turned to look in the direction of the theatre. Something caused the woman to scream and collapse, but before she could hit the glass window, her partner caught her and lowered her gently to the footpath. There were more screams and people started to run past the window, fear visible on each one of their faces.

A man walked in front of the window carrying a woman who Isaac had assumed had also fainted, but after watching them travel past, he realised that the man's face was buried in the girls neck and he wasn't watching where he was walking. The man was wearing a brown and red suit and the woman in his arms had on a strange blue and brown dress. Both were soaked through from the heavy rain outside. He didn't recognise them, as the man pushed his way passed the people outside, and entered the restaurant. The waiter who had served Isaac the drink, tried to stop the man from entering, but he just pushed past him, and stopped in the doorway to the dining room. Isaac couldn't see the man's face, as it was buried into the neck of the woman, but when his blood soaked face lifted up from the girls neck, and started looking around, the room seemed to fall out from under him, as James face came into view. The tear streaked face scanned the room looking for someone. When it fell upon Isaac he watched the eyes roll up into the man's head and he collapsed on top of the girl like a marionette whose strings had been cut. Without giving the other patrons of the restaurant a second thought, he pushed his way through the room (his chair sent skittering across the room and hitting another patron who was watching the unfolding events), pushing over any diner who got in his way.

Isaac slowed as he approached the couple on the floor, pushing restaurant staff and patrons aside, and lifted the man off the girl, with a gasp, he realised the man, was indeed, his future son-in-law, James, and the woman was his daughter Eleanor. The man'-

s eyes rolled back and his lips started to move. Isaac moved his ear to James' lips and heard the faintest whisper of the word "Lycanthrope" before he passed out again. With some help, Isaac lifted James off of his daughter and laid him to one side, he was unconscious, but still breathing so Isaac turned his attention back to Eleanor. Her skin was incredibly pale and her eyes were closed. As he looked to the side of her face he found a large jagged wound on her shoulder, he looked at it un-comprehending what he was actually seeing, before his mind broke through haze that had settled in his brain and he realised that the brown of her dress was blood that had come from the wound in her shoulder. There was a woman's scream followed by a crash and Isaac turned around to see a waiter fanning a towel over the screaming woman, who had collapsed.

"Is there a doctor in the place?" Isaac called out

"I'm a doctor," a rotund gentleman replied pushing through the crowd, as he approached and looked at the couple on the floor, he stopped and held a hand in front of his face. "Oh god," said the doctor, crossing a hand across his chest, "we need to get her away from the other patrons, is there another, more private room, we can move her to?" he asked turning to one of the restaurant staff.

"This way, there is a spare room in the back." came the voice of the manager who was waving for some of the staff to come and help move her.

With all due care, the manager and staff carried Eleanor out of the main room, followed by the doctor. Isaac was about to follow when he felt a hand on his shoulder, "best not Sir, if there is anything that can be done to help her they will need all the space in the room." Isaac spun around, and was about to hit the man restraining him, when he noticed the man was a soldier with sorrow in his eyes.

"What am I supposed to do, she is my only child." Isaac responded, turning back to the door, "I can't just stand here, if I can't see to my daughter, I need to find whoever did this."

"Do you know anyone who might have a reason to attack them?" the soldier asked.

Isaac was about to reply, when a red faced police constable walked through the main entrance, he looked toward James laid out on the floor and his face drained of all colour as he recognised the red puddle on the floor where Eleanor had lain. Isaac felt something brush his ankle and he looked down to see James looking up at him. Isaac knelt down and noticed that James eyes didn't follow, but looked up to the ceiling. Isaac realised, from the faraway expression, that James wasn't focused on the ceiling, he was watching visions only seen within his minds eye.

Isaac eyes filled with tears. "Please James, tell me what has happened, who attacked you?"

For the second time, James lips moved, but again only one word escaped his lips before his eyes closed and his head fell to the side. "What did he say?" the constable asked.

Isaac stood up and looked the constable in the eyes, "a monster attacked them."

"Where were they coming from when they were attacked?" asked the constable

"I brought them tickets to tonight's show at the theatre. They were on their way here to meet me for dinner to celebrate their engagement." Isaac replied looking toward the door where his daughter had been taken.

The door opened and out stepped the doctor without his jacket, followed by the manager whose face was pale, he ordered two glasses of brandy, handed one to the doctor and one to Isaac. "Please sir, take a seat." Isaac was about to push past when he felt a hand on his shoulder gently push him into the seat, and the glass pressed into his hand.

"I am sorry to tell you Sir, but your daughter died from blood loss," the doctor stated taking a deep drink from his own glass, Isaac looked the doctor in his eyes hoping that he was wrong, he had seen her pale skin, the wound on her shoulder and the blood on her dress, but still hoped she was alive. The doctor shook his head and handed the empty glass back to the manager. Tugging up his trousers, he crouched down and started to examine James, after asking for help to remove James' jacket, he began his examination. When he had finished, he looked up at Isaac with surprise and confusion on his face. "Did you say that you knew this young man?"

"He is, was," Isaac corrected himself, "engaged to be married to my daughter."

"Sir, she must have meant a lot to both of you as he was is serious pain from carrying her to you."

"What do you mean?"

"He has a broken arm and several broken ribs. He needs to get to a hospital quickly to receive medical attention. He must have used every fibre of his being to get here, it's amazing that he managed to get here at all."

Isaac scowled at him, anger rolling inside, "he promised to give his life to protect her." Isaac looked away from James and back to the room where Eleanor lay. "What will happen to my daughter now?"

"The detectives will want to see her, but I am afraid that she will be taken to the morgue. You need to think about making funeral arrangements for her."

Isaac's fingers twitched and the glass fell, as if in slow motion to the floor, bounced then shattered as it hit the floor for a second time, scattering shards in a wide circle "Are you ok, Sir?" the doctor asked, "is there any family you can stay with?"

Isaac looked him in the eyes, shaking his head. "No, she was my only child, all I have left is my house staff."

"Where do you live?" the soldier, who had remained by Isaac's side, asked.

Isaac whispered the address and the soldier helped him to his feet. The constable was about to stop them when the soldier held out his hand. "I, and my companion will make sure he gets home and attend to the house staff. If it helps, I will also stay in the house until an inspector arrives in the morning."

The constable allowed them leave, before summoning an ambulance to take the boy to the hospital, and the girl to the morgue.

Chapter IV
Initial Investigation.

The Black Maria pulled up outside the restaurant next to a white hospital carriage, its passengers, consisting of a contingent of police constables, climbed down and spread out to search the area. As the first of the constables reached the alley where the murder had taken place, a second Maria pulled up and out climbed it's compliment of constables. When the constables spread out, following their colleagues, two detective climbed out, but before climbing down, the oldest stood up straight and took a look around from the top step to get a better view above people's heads. He looked up to the cloud covered sky and was grateful for the break in the rain as he climbed down from the carriage. Being mindful of the nearly washed away blood stain in front of the door, he stepped over the blood, and being careful not to touch the door handle, he pushed through the door and entered the restaurant.

The detective looked around at the blood that covered the lobby area and doorway leaving a visible trail. Looking back over his shoulder, out into the street, beyond the door, the rain had nearly obliterated the blood trail between here and the scene of the crime. Inside, he observed a young man being lifted onto a stretcher on his way to hospital.

"My name is Detective Brass, who is this and where is the body that was reported?" he asked looking around at the staff and diners, still sat around the room. A gentleman stepped forward introduced himself as a Doctor and, as he held his hand out to a back room indicating that the detective should follow.

"We moved her to a back room to see if I could do anything to save her."

"If I may ask, who are you, Sir, and what have you got to do with this?"

"My name is, Doctor Montgomery Silver, I was having dinner here when the boy came in, covered in blood, carrying the poor girl's dead body." he explained as he lead the detective through a corridor to the back room.

"Do you know who the boy is?"

"According to the girl's father, the boy's name is James Purcell, he was the girl's fiancée," the doctor replied as he lead the detective through the door into another room.

"And how do you know that the girl is dead and not mortally wounded, Doctor?" The detective asked, following the doctor to where a body lay covered in a white linen tablecloth. Brass looked over the cover on the body and noticed that there was only a little blood soaked into the lower half of the sheet, but not around the upper area.

Doctor Silver pulled the white tablecloth away from the girls head and face, with all the due reverence he would have given to his own child. Her face was deathly pale and almost the same colour of the sheet. He looked up at the detective who was still waiting for positive proof, with a sigh, he carefully folded the sheet down across her chest then carefully peeled the blood stained clothing away from the gaping wound in her shoulder. The detective turned away, his face turning green and promptly was sick on the floor. The doctor plucked a napkin from a pile on a cupboard and handed it to the detective to wipe his face before explaining his findings. Once the detective regained control of his faculties and his former facial colour, the doctor started to explain. "Judging by the nature of the wound in her shoulder, it would have meant that she had lost a lot of blood very, very quickly.", he said before replacing the sheet back over the girl's face.

"What would be the cause of such an injury?"

"Detective, this is not caused by a man with any kind of weapon, this type of wound can only be caused by a wild animal biting down on her shoulder from above and then pulling the skin and muscle underneath away."

"And how are you able to tell that, Doctor?"

"The edges of the wound are torn and there are wolves, or dog like teeth marks on the lowest edges. I saw too many injuries when I worked in Africa, not to recognise a of wound of this kind."

The detective could feel his stomach turning cartwheels and decided to change the subject. "Do you know the name of the girl laid on this table?"

"Yes, Detective, her name is Eleanor Theologian."

"And how do you know of this?"

"They were coming here to meet the girl's father, Professor Isaac Theologian, for dinner to celebrate their engagement. It was he who told me this."

"And what of the Professor, where is he now?"

"We believed that it would be better for him to be taken home. A soldier and his companion have taken him back to his home and have offered to stay with him until you arrived."

"Do you have his address?"

"Yes, Detective," he said putting his hand in his waistcoat pocket and pulling out a piece of paper. "Would you mind if I accompanied you to his house, via a detour to my surgery to collect some items that may be of assistance to him."

"Of course, Doctor, but may I ask if you would you be willing to testify as to the cause of death in any kind of hearing or trial?"

"Detective, I would consider it my duty to help out in any way to bring to justice whatever caused the poor girls death."

The detective nodded and started walking towards the door. "What about the boy, this James Purcell?"

"He has a broken arm and several broke ribs. I am amazed that he made it here carrying her body with his injuries. One of your constables is accompanying him to the hospital where he can receive more care, than I can offer him in my own surgery."

Anything else you can tell me about his condition, any kind of injuries that matched hers?"

"It's hard to tell without a proper medical examination of him, as he was covered in the girl's blood that had mixed with the rain water."

"Thank you, Doctor," the detective said as he opened the door and headed back into the restaurant. "I need to investigate the murder site, then I will be back to collect you."

"I'm not going anywhere, well, not until someone comes to take the girl's body to the morgue." the doctor replied as he watched the detective head out of the door and out of the restaurant, into the night.

Before he left the restaurant, Detective Brass turned to one of the constables near the door, "I want statements from everyone in here tonight and I will need them to come back tomorrow for an initial inquiry into what happened." The constable nodded to confirm his orders then turned to pass the orders to his fellows. Detective Brass walked back out into the night and headed towards the alleyway where the murder took place, and realised that the rain was slowly starting again, the trail had nearly been washed away and would not survive until daylight. He caught up with his colleague just inside the entrance to the alley beside the theatre. "What have you found, Mr. Cobbler?" he asked watching constables walk around shining lanterns around in the dark.

"There are signs of a struggle and what's left of a large puddle of blood, but no weapon." Cobbler watched Brass looking thought the gloom before asking him a question. "You have seen the victim, Sir?"

"Yes Mr. Cobbler, she died of a large wound to her shoulder that severed one of her major arteries." Brass stated as he watched the search.

"And that was bad sir?"

"A doctor in the restaurant said that the artery allows massive amounts of blood to circulate around the body, when it was severed, the poor girl would have suffered from exsanguination in a very short time."

"Did he say what could have caused the wound?"

"The doctor said that it was caused by a wild animal."

"How would he know that?"

"He used to work in Africa, and had experience dealing with people who had suffered from animal attacks."

"Do you believe him, Sir?"

"I do not know of a wild animal that could have caused it, and there have been no report's of anyone having seen one roaming the streets."

"A wild animal, Sir?"

"He said that judging from the tearing to the edges of the wound, some kind of wild animal had bitten down on her from above."

"Is that even possible?"

Detective Brass continued to watch the constables searching the area, his stomach was already turning at the thought of so much blood that would be around, after taking a deep breath, the two of them walked into the alley that was illuminated by several lanterns being carried by constable's. Detective Brass took a lantern from the closest constable and shone it up along the walls of the building on either side of the lane. The walls were clear of any ledges or platforms that could have been used by any kind of animal to pounce from, but he felt that there was something amiss. As he walked along the cobbled ground, looking for clues, he was stopped by Mr. Cobbler as they neared the middle.

"This is where she was killed," Cobbler said pointing to what remained of the blood pooled blood that had gathered between the stones.

As he looked about he knew that there was very little that could be done to find whoever, or whatever, had attacked the two and killed the girl.

"Do you think that there may be more to this?"

"I do not know Cobbler, have you found anything that could have been used as a weapon?"

"Do you think that the boy could be responsible?"

"Do you know about the boy?" Detective Brass asked confused.

"I questioned all of the people that were still in the area, and I watched as he was loaded into the carriage that would take him to the hospital."

"Did they see anyone enter or leave the alley?"

"No one entered or left either end of the alleyway."

"So all we have is the boy as our only suspect," Brass said trying to take his eyes off the blood, "Finish up here, I need to speak to the father of the girl. Once I am done we will go and see to the boy. Make sure that no one can enter this area until I am finished here."

"Yes, Sir."

Detective Brass turned away from the blood and left the alley. When he reached the restaurant, he was stopped as men, carrying the girl's body on a stretcher, came out. He walked over to their carriage and opened the door for them. He watched them secure her inside, climb back out and then climb up into the front and drive away. A Hackney Carriage pulled up and Brass ordered the driver to wait while he went inside. The doctor already had his coat and hat on when Brass came back in, and after a nod, they both walked out, climbed into the waiting carriage and headed for the doctors surgery.

The carriage pulled outside the doctor's surgery and Brass followed him inside. While the doctor set about finding his bag and solutions, he may need to help the girl's father, Detective Brass looked around the various African souvenirs that the doctor had lined the walls with.

"Did you shoot all these animals, Doctor?" Brass asked looking up at a tiger's head.

The doctor stopped his search and walked out to the waiting room, "some of them, yes, but most were a gift along with the other African items."

"Do you own a hunting rifle?" queried Brass.

"Somewhere, but I don't think it is the time for this kind of discussion." He replied and finished packing his bag. After locking the surgery back up, they climbed back into the carriage and travelled out to the house of Professor Isaac Theologian.

The journey out to the village was only a short trip, but it gave the doctor long enough to tell Brass about one of his African adventures. By the time the story had come to an end, the carriage had made its way through several small villages in the surrounding hills and valley and had come to a stop outside a house. Detective Brass climbed out and looked around. Most of the houses in the village were small, with one or two larger buildings scattered around. The one they now stood outside of was not the largest in the village, but was one of the biggest in the immediate area. "Is this the correct place?" Brass asked the driver.

"This is the address you gave me, Detective." the driver replied with a yawn.

The detective looked back up to the door, and pulling his coat tight around to shield himself from the rain, headed through the gate and up the path with the doctor trailing behind. As they reached the front door, it was opened by a manservant who was watching them.

"And you gentleman are?" the manservant asked.

"Detective Brass and Doctor Silvers, we are here to see Professor Isaac Theologian."

"What about Mistress Eleanor and Master James?"

"I don't know if I should be discussing that with you." Brass responded.

"My wife and I have served the family for most of our lives, if something is wrong, then it's my job to receive the messages and give them to the Professor." the manservant said looking down his nose at the detective.

"Will you let us in if I tell you?"

The manservant didn't answer, just nodded.

After taking a deep breath, Detective Brass spoke up, "the Professor's daughter, Eleanor, has been killed, and James Purcell is now in hospital under police guard."

"You think that the young master is responsible for killing the Professor's daughter?"

"I won't lie, but at present, he is our only suspect."

The manservant looked at him for a few moments then stepped aside, "can I take your coats and hats?" The doctor put down his bag, took off his coat and passed it to the manservant, along with his hat. When the detective had also passed his own coat and hat over, the manservant lead them into the study.

Detective Brass looked around the room taking in the shelves of books and walls lined with paintings and diagrams. At one end behind the desk near the fire, there were three high back chairs. In one of the chairs was a soldier and next to him sat a woman. Brass suspected this was the couple who had offered to take the Professor home, who he suspected was the older gentleman in the last seat. He walked over and coughed to interrupt their conversation. "Professor Isaac Theologian?" he asked, looking towards the old man who was sat there quietly holding a glass of amber fluid, looking into a fire with water filled red eyes. The old gentleman looked up to confirm his theory.

Brass was about to ask a question when the doctor interrupted, "would you mind taking the two guest into another room to ask your questions, I would like to check on the Professor in private." Brass nodded and escorted the soldier and his companion out and across the hall to the dining room opposite. Once they were in and seated, the doors were closed by the manservant.

Detective Brass asked the couple about what they had seen and heard at the restaurant. He wrote down everything he was told and then when they were finished, he asked them about what the Professor may have said while they were with him. When they had finished telling him everything they knew, Brass thanked them and let them leave. He watched as the manservant fetched their coats and hailed them a cab. As the cab pulled away, the study door opened and the doctor came out. "You can see him now, but don't ask too many questions. As soon as your done, I am going to give him something to help him sleep tonight," he said and led Brass back in. Isaac was stood glaring at the fire and didn't turn until the detective cleared his throat.

"I am sorry for your loss, but I need to ask you some questions while the events are still fresh in your memory." Brass started, when the Professor didn't respond, he continued, "is there anyone you know of that may have a reason to kill your daughter?"

Isaac looked away from the fire and over to his shelves, "take a look around, I am sure that during my work I have trampled on someone's toes, but I don't know about anyone who has taken it personally enough to want to attack me or my daughter."

"What about the boy, James Purcell?"

"What about him?"

"Would he have anything to gain from killing her?"

Isaac's faced turned dark, "I don't care if he killed her or not, he promised to give his life to protect her in exchange for my permission to marry. He is still alive and she isn't, he failed to keep his promise, so is as much responsible as whoever did kill her."

"Witnesses said he spoke something before passing out, what did he say?"

"He said a monster killed her."

"A monster, is that everything?"

"That was all."

Brass looked at him for a few minutes in silence, but after a glare from the doctor, decided that he had troubled the Professor enough. He thanked the Professor then walked out to the lobby with the doctor in tow.

"Did you get the information you wanted Detective?"

"He is not telling me everything, but it's getting late."

"Are you heading back to the area?" asked the doctor.

"Yes."

"Would you mind waiting while I see the Professor to bed?"

"Of course not, Doctor." Brass replied and watched as the doctor nodded to the manservant, then re-entered the study.

With the help of the manservant, Professor Isaac was taken up to bed. The doctor gave him something to help him sleep and when the Professor was settled, the doctor came back down stairs, collected his items, joined the detective and they rode back to Bristol.

Chapter V
Waking up in Hospital.

Something caused me to wake from a deep dreamless sleep, a feeling that I was supposed to be doing an important task played on my mind. My mind was cloudy and consciousness was slowly pushing through. A crash of metal on a tiled floor caused my mind to sharply snap into focus and my eyes to open. As quick as they opened, I shut them again. With the sharp wake-up came the even sharper pain and a cry escaped my lips. I took a deep breath and my chest filled with pain that started from one side to the other. Whatever had happened to me had left me in a bad condition, but what struck me most was that my last memory was a blur, as if looking through a dirty window. When the pain had subsided enough, I slowly opened my eyes and found myself looking up to an unfamiliar ceiling. I lay there trying to work out where I could be.

"So, you have finally decided to wake up then?" a voice asked from my left hand side.

"Where am I?"

"You are in a hospital, Mr. Purcell," came the reply. I tilted my head to look at a constable that was stood next to my bed.

"What am I doing here?"

"You don't remember?" the constable asked without looking at me.

Suddenly, memories started to slowly filter back

"I remember that my fiancée and I had been to the theatre and were attacked as we passed an alley. I have a vague memory of trying to stop the attacker, but was thrown into a wall and knocked unconscious."

"You don't remember the restaurant?"

"The restaurant where we were supposed to meet up with Professor Isaac?"

The constable was about to answer when another crash caused us both to turn towards the middle of the room. The sudden move caused me to instantly feel dizzy, but when my vision stopped spinning, I found myself looking at a doctor and nurse putting things on a trolley.

"Is that Professor Isaac Theologian that you are referring to?" continued the constable, searching his pockets for a pencil and notepad.

"Who else would it be?" I replied, but a wave of pain made the reply sound aggressive. "Has he, or Eleanor, been to see me since I was brought here?"

"Since you walked into the restaurant carrying his dead daughter's body, he has not been anywhere near you."

"Are you sure she is dead?" I cried out

The constable looked down at me with one eyebrow raised. "I need to report to my station that you are now awake. The detectives that are investigating the incident will need to talk to you.", he said before heading for the foot of the bed. As he passed by, he turned to look back at me. "Do not try to leave the hospital, we are not quite finished talking to you." he added, before turning to the door and leaving.

I tried to sit up to get a better look around, but a fresh wave of pain warned me against the action and I collapsed back onto the bed. A nurse must have seen me as I heard footsteps approaching before one appeared by my bed. She was wearing a blue dress with white collar and cuffs, but had a white apron over the front. "Can I help you, is there something you need?" she asked with a big friendly smile.

"How long have I been in here?"

"You have been asleep since you came in here two days ago."

"Have I had any visitors?" I asked licking my dry lips.

She poured water into a tin cup and held it up to my lips so I could drink. "Apart from the police, you have had no visitors at all.", she said taking the empty cup away and putting it back on the cupboard beside the bed.

Two days, I thought to myself, looking around the room, no wonder I feel thirsty. "Can I have some more water, please?" She filled the cup up again and helped me drink it. By the time I had finished, the constable had come back, but he was now accompanied by two other gentlemen.

"This is Detective Brass and Detective Cobbler, they are investigating the murder of your fiancée," the constable stated, pointing to each of the gentlemen as he said their names.

"Thank you constable," the older of the two said, from the foot of my bed. "Mr. Purcell, do you feel up to answering a few questions about what happened?" he asked pulling out a notebook.

"While you were unconscious, we held an inquiry to see if we could work out what happened from witness statements. Apart from you and Eleanor Theologian, no one entered or exited the alley where you were attacked. Can you tell me the events as you remember them, please?"

I described everything that I could remember and watched as he made copious notes. By the time I had finished, I was feeling hungry and very thirsty. I reached for the jug of water beside the bed and doubled over as pain from the ribs, that I had forgotten were broken, protested against the movement. The nurse must have seen my attempt as she returned, refilled the cup and helped me sit up to drink it. Once I had finished and the nurse had returned to her other charges, the questions started again.

"What can you tell me of your attacker?"

The image of the werewolf was permanently stuck in my mind and I wondered how to describe it without sounding crazy. I looked at the detective who was waiting for an answer and took in a deep pain filled breath that caused my broken ribs grind together. "He was larger than me by a head and a half, had broad shoulders like someone who was used to heavy lifting and had dark skin." It was the only way I could think of describing something that most people believed only existed in a horror story.

"The police surgeon stated that the wound, that killed your fiancée, was caused by an animal that resembles a large dog or a wolf, do you remember if the attacker had an animal with him that matched what he described?"

I looked at him and immediately started to describe the werewolf, leaving out the fact it walked on two legs. "It was too dark to get a good look, but it had dark and light fur, and had eyes that glowed gold like flames that sat on each side of a muzzle that ran slick with rain and foam. The look of expectation on it's face was forever etched on my mind and it terrified me. When Eleanor passed out, I tried to attack the wolf, but the wolf was quicker and knocked me into the wall of the alley."

Detective Brass nodded as took notes, while Detective Cobbler seemed to be trying to work out from my body language if I was lying or not. "That would match up with the paw prints that we found in the alley. We found two blood trails in the alley, one made by you, as you carried Eleanor to the restaurant, the other lead towards the opposite end, but disappeared after a few steps. The rain that night had washed a lot of the blood away by the time we arrived, and by morning, it was all gone."

"When can I get out of here?" I called out to a doctor who was walking past.

"If you can walk out of here, you don't need to remain here." he replied only casting me the slightest of glances.

"Where will you go?" Detective Brass asked.

"Back to Professor Isaac's house first then I will see what happens from there.", I said looking for my clothes. "I hate hospitals and need to get out of here regardless of whatever state I am in, before I catch something that will make me sick".

The doctor stopped what he was doing, looked at me seeing I was serious about getting out of the place. "Mr. Purcell," he started, his voice filled with authority, "you have quite a few broken ribs and a broken arm, if it's going to heal without causing you problems in the future, you are going to need to be kept bandaged up and not move about."

"Where are my clothes?" I asked ignoring what he said.

"They were covered in blood and have been taken as evidence."

"As evidence of what?"

"As evidence that you are the actual killer!"

"Me!" I yelled, silencing all conversations in the room and earning several disapproving looks, "but I loved her, we were to be married and take over Professor Isaac's research for the University. Why would I want to kill her, what would I possibly gain from killing her. I owe them my life.", I said in a more hushed tone.

"That is the question that needs to be answered. If we cannot find your attacker then it looks like you could be the prime suspect in this case." Brass replied watching me.

"Is there someone that can be contacted who can bring you fresh clothes and take you home?" the doctor interrupted.

"Everything I own is at Isaac's house." I replied

"It would not be wise to go back there as he holds you responsible for her death."

"I have to go back there, I have to talk to him."

"I will send one of the porters to deal with it." the doctor said, turning to one who had just entered.

"I think it is time that you wrap up the questions and leave him in peace.", he said to the detectives.

"Is there any other place you can go, should you find yourself unwelcome there?" asked Detective Brass.

"There is my parent's house near the docks, but I will probably get a room somewhere." I gave him my parent's address and with a thank you, he wrote it down on his pad and put the pad away.

"One more thing, do not try to leave the area as it will make you look more guilty." He nodded to the constable and all three of them left.

A few hours later, the porter returned with a friendly, familiar face who walked in through the door carrying a bag. I smiled weakly as Isaac's manservant walked towards me after thanking the porter.

"Master James, it's good to see you up after all that has happened." He said, stepping up to the bed and helping me get out. After about twenty minutes of wrestling, I was dressed with the exception off my broken arm that was bandaged up under my shirt. Isaac's man helped me out of the hospital and into the carriage waiting in the yard to take us back to the place I had called home for the last few years.

Chapter VI
Goodbye Isaac.

"Isaac, I'm sorry." was all I could say before a glass flew towards me, before shattering against the wall behind.

"How could you, how dare you show your face here, I trusted you to keep her safe, you promised to give your life to protect her!" Isaac screamed at me from across the room.

I did not know what I was expecting when I left the hospital, but to be attacked with such a verbal tirade, along with flying objects, as soon as I entered the front door was not at the top of my list. I suppose I should have expected some sort of outburst from him as he was grieving for the loss of his daughter's life, but this, this seemed almost out of control.

"Isaac what could I have done, we were attacked by a Lycanthrope." I protested, as I watched him search for something else to use as a weapon to throw at me.

"You should have attacked it, you should have thrown your own worthless life at the monster to save her!"

"Isaac, I tried, that's how I ended up with these injuries."

"You didn't try hard enough."

"What is going on Isaac, it said the reason it attacked us, was to kill her and make me watch!" I yelled back at him.

"I don't know what your talking about. All I care about is that she should be here and you should be dead!"

I stood in the doorway of the study in front of Isaac. After much arguing and protesting, the hospital had released me into Isaac's manservant's care, my body was covered in scratches and bruises, my ribs bandaged up where several had been broken and one of my arms in a sling, where the lower arm had been fractured. The police had left the hospital allowing me to leave, but from the expression on the face of the detectives, they believed that I was the killer. I tried to explain to Isaac what had happened that night, I tried again to protest my innocence, and that I was lucky to be alive. Isaac and myself were most eminent of specialists in this kind of thing, but Isaac ignored all of this and continued his verbal tirade towards me. Isaac was still screaming at me, but I realised that I was ignoring him, lost in my own thoughts, tears threatening to break out.

"Isaac," I said trying to interrupt him, but he continued on, "Isaac, if you will not let me defend myself I will get my stuff and leave."

"Go, get your stuff, get out of my house, I don't ever want to see you again!" he shouted. I was about to say something else, but he turned around to look into the fire that burned in his study and acted like he was the only one in the room. I stood there hoping for another chance to defend myself, to persuade Isaac that it wasn't my fault, but when none came, I turned around, walked out of the study and over to the stairs. As I started climbing up, the manservant stopped me.

"Master James?"

"I'm going up to my room to get as much of my stuff that I can carry and then I'm leaving. Isaac doesn't want me here anymore."

"Please give him time, he needs to mourn Eleanor."

"We both loved her and should be together, not falling apart."

"I am sure he will accept you back if you give him some space for a while."

"I know, I agree that we all need some space for a while.", I said walking up the stairs. I put my hand in my pocket and pulled out a piece of paper with an address on it. "I have family in Bristol that I can stay with. If you need to contact me, you can find me here."

"I will keep it safe.", he said taking the paper and putting it in his pocket."Will you be ok on your own?" he asked holding out a hand to steady me as I started swaying on the stairs.

"I just need to sit down. As to Isaac, I fear that he may go off and do something stupid.", I said as I stepped onto the landing and headed down the corridor to my room. I opened my room's door, entered and reaching under the bed, pulled out a bag. "If he goes after the monster that killed Eleanor, he will be killed by it as well."

"Is it one of those species that you have been studying for the University?" he asked, carefully removing my clothes from various drawers around the room.

"Yes, it's a very dangerous one, I don't understand why it didn't kill both of us, after all it had every chance, but ..."

"You have been badly injured, Sir.", he said, moving over to the wardrobe and taking out items to put into another bag.

"I think there is something else going on here, as the monster was a Lycanthrope."

"A werewolf sir?"

"Yes, a werewolf, they are not known for leaving survivors unless they want something from that person." I said picking up my University work and dropping it in a satchel.

"What will you do while you are away?" The manservant asked closing up my bags and taking them over to set at the door.

"I'll go see the Head of the University tomorrow and see if I can continue the work on my own."

"Do you think he will allow it?"

"I do not know, I can only try." I replied as we walked out of my room.

The manservant placed my bags on the floor and pulled a key out of his jacket pocket. He locked the door and returned the key before picking up the bags and leading the way back down the stairs. I looked into the study as we passed, but Isaac refused to look at me. We headed down to the kitchen to see the manservant's wife, and Isaac's cook, to say goodbye.

She was working on a meal, when we entered the room, and as she looked up to me I could see that her eyes were full of sadness and were red from where she had been crying. She shook the flour off her hands, from the bread she had been making, wiped her hands on her apron and walked over to give me a gentle hug.

"You not leaving, are you Master James?" she asked looking me up and down.

"Isaac does not want me in the house any more. I think we all need some space for a while."

"Are you going to be ok, if you need somewhere to stay, you can always spend a night at ours." she offered

"I will be ok," I said smiling weakly, "I was just saying that I have friends and family I can stay with."

"Well, if your sure, but if you ever need a bit of help, you can come to us"", she said, softly smiling and giving me another hug.

"Do you want me to arrange for a carriage?" Isaacs manservant asked.

"No, thank you, I am sure I can find one.", I said shaking his hand.

"Goodbye, Master James." the manservant said opening the front door.

"Goodbye." I replied before walking out of the door.

With my bags slung over my good arm, I walked down the garden path, casting a last glance up at the house, before starting down the road headed for Bristol. As I walked, I started to weigh up my options and attempted to draw up some plans for my future. Without Isaac, and support from the University, I had no job or any kind of income. If I was going to support myself I would have to consider finding work. When I stopped to look around, I realised that I had walked further along the road than I thought I would, but nowhere far enough to get be to my destination.

"Need a lift, mate?" ma voice called out, and I turned around to see a horse drawn cart behind me.

"Are you heading into Bristol?" I asked looking up to the driver.

"Heading for Bedminster in South Bristol, will that do you?" he asked.

"That would be fine with me as long as your happy with it."", I said smiling back. The driver secured the reins and pulled on the brakes. Taking my bags and placing them on the back, he helped me up onto the bench next to his seat and together we rode into Bristol. Darkness was creeping up behind us and by the time we had reached the more central areas, close to the docklands, the lamp lighters were already out lighting the gas street lamps. The cart driver turned onto a road that started following the river towards where the shipping and warehousing buildings were to be found. The cart pulled up outside a gate and the owner jumped down and helped me get off.

"Do you live around here?" he asked, fetching my bags off the back of his cart.

"Not far."

"If you don't mind waiting while I unload, I can give you a ride the rest of the way to your house."

"Thanks for the offer, but I can manage, my destination is really not far away.", I said with a grunt as I hoisted my bags up and onto my shoulder.

"Someone waiting for you?"

"Parent's will be home."

"Well good luck then mate.", he said as the gates opened. He jumped up onto the carriage and drove it on through the gates, into the yard.

I watched the gates close before heading back along the road towards my parent's home. Despite the warm glow from the gas lights, the mist rolling in from the river made the air cold and damp, my injuries were starting to ache and I really wanted to get to the house quickly. I passed another dockyard gate and heard voices coming from inside. Even though its was obvious that most were tired from a long days work, the voices were in high spirits. I stepped into the shadows to hide and watched as a group of men, the owners of the voices, exited through a doorway in the gate of the nearest yard and walk down the road. Once they were past I stepped out of my hiding place and continued down the road. I had made it several yards when I felt a hand on my shoulder.

"What's a highly educated boy like you doing in a place like this?" came a tired, old voice.

I spun around and looked up into the stern eyes of my father and nearly fell to my knees. My bags fell to the ground and I felt him grab me, hoisting me back up onto my feet. After a few minutes my knees stopped trembling enough to allow me to stand on my own. Eventually I built up the nerve to speak, After all the stories about me being a suspected killer, I didn't know what to say. "Hello Father, do you mind if I stay with you and Mother for a bit until I can find my own place?"

He held me in a firm grip, looking at me with those commanding eyes of his before answering. "Just answer me one question before I answer yours. Did you kill the girl, Eleanor Theologian?"

His eyes never left mine and I could feel tears welling up in my own eyes, I kept on looking into his for a few minutes before answering with just one single small word. "No."

His eyes kept fixed on me, until a gentle smile broke his stern features "I didn't think so.", he said before reaching down and grabbing my bags. We walked on down the road towards the family home. On the way I told him everything about my life over the past few months since we had last spoken, the only thing I didn't tell him about was the same thing that I had kept from the police. I told him the same story that I had told to the police, right down to the description of the killer, that I had made up. A few blocks short of the house he stopped me.

"That's not what happened is it?", he had grabbed my shoulder in a vice like grip and forced me to turn around, "it's one of those monsters you have been chasing?"

I could not lie to him, as he would see right through it, the fact that he was asking me this, proved that he knew different. "If people knew the truth they would think I was even more guilty, and then think I was crazy." I replied.

He didn't say anything as we carried on walking towards the house. As we passed through the gate he stopped me and asked me to wait outside while he went on in alone. He walked into the house, but left the door open enough for me to hear what was going on inside. I could hear a hushed conversation between him and my mother, but continued to wait. It went quite for a few minutes before the door opened and my mother appeared at the door, we stood there looking at each other and I could see tears on her face, I took a step towards her and she threw her arms around me and burst out crying.

"Are you going to stand there all night crying while everyone watches?" my father said, trying to separate us enough to get us inside.

Once were were all inside, along with the bags I had brought with me, mother fussed about the small kitchen to get fathers dinner. "Have you had any-thing to eat yet?" she ask.

"No, not since I left the hospital." The truth was that I had probably not eaten in several days.

Whatever she had cooked in the pot was shared out between us and after finishing it off I retold everything that had happened to my mother. The round up of events took nearly an hour, plus with all the questions they asked afterwards I felt like I had been drained of all energy. Father pulled out a pock-et watch, looked at the clock on the sideboard, ad-justed the time then with a click, closed the watch and stood up.

"You look like you're in need of a good drink.", father said, mother had gone out to the kitchen to clean up, he followed her out and told her that he was taking me down to the pub. He picked up my coat, helped me put it on, before getting his own on as we prepared to head out into the night.

Chapter VII
Whispers of Distrust and Fear.

High upon the gallows tree swung the noble-hearted three.

By the vengeful tyrant stricken in their bloom;

But they met him face to face, with the courage of their race,

And they went with souls undaunted to their doom.

"God save Ireland!" said the heroes;

"God save Ireland" said they all.

Whether on the scaffold high

Or the battlefield we die,

Oh, what matter when for Erin dear we fall! 1

Girt around with cruel foes, still their courage proudly rose,

For they thought of hearts that loved them far and near;

Of the millions true and brave o'er the ocean's swelling wave,

And the friends in holy Ireland ever dear.

"God save Ireland!" said the heroes;

"God save Ireland" said they all.

Whether on the scaffold high

Or the battlefield we die,

Oh, what matter when for Erin dear we fall!

Climbed they up the rugged stair, rang their voices out in
prayer,

Then with England's fatal cord around them cast,

Close beside the gallows tree kissed like brothers lovingly,

True to home and faith and freedom to the last.

"God save Ireland!" said the heroes;

"God save Ireland" said they all.

Whether on the scaffold high

Or the battlefield we die,

Oh, what matter when for Erin dear we fall!

God Save ireland.
Written by Timothy Daniel Sullivan 1867

The pub on the corner of the street was exactly as I remembered it as a child. An Irish Community had built up around this area, and the pub catered to the dock workers and their families. Under the orange glow of the street lamps, the outside seemed to be painted brown and cream with a sign above the door bearing a picture of a pike and fishing rod. I looked up to the sign above the windows and found the name pike and fishing rod painted in what could be gold. Music was coming from inside and I listened to it as we approached the front door. It had been a few years since I had heard the song, but I instantly recognised the lyrics "god save Ireland" being shouted moments before the sound of a scuffle. A few moments later, a pair of burly men were thrown out of the door, followed by a crowd. The minute they were on their feet, they went back to knocking seven bells out of each other, no doubt fuelled on by the cheering and taunts from the crowd.

"I know that I have been away for a while, but is this normal?"

"Well, let's just say, if the Peelers don't show up, they will be back to work in the morning, both sporting black eye's, hangovers and the best of friends again." He looked around at the crowd then back to the fighters, "that is assuming that the fighting doesn't get out of hand and one of the ejits doesn't kill the other." he shrugged, turned back to the door, pushed his way past the crowd and into the pub.

I was hoping that there wouldn't be much of a crowd inside, as I didn't want to risk any further bangs to my already bruised and broken body. Looking around, the first thing to hit me was the thick cloud of smoke that floated towards the rafters, to me it looked like fog had rolled in through the front door and become trapped. The gas lamps around the walls cast the room in a yellow glow that seemed to be amplified by the isolated weather pattern of smoke on the ceiling. We pushed our way to the bar and the volume in the room dropped enough for me to hear people whispering.

"It's him, isn't it."

"Got to be."

"Is that Purcell's boy?"

"Must be hitting them hard to know that their son is a murderer."

"Look at the skinny little runt, there is no way that he could have done it!"

"The paper said that there were many witnesses that spotted him enter after the woman, then shortly after he came out with her dead body."

"What about the restaurant, what about all those people that were there and watched him enter?"

I didn't realise that my father had stopped until I walked into his back. There was a tremor in his arms and I realised that he was doing his best to control his anger. "I don't want to cause any trouble, let's go somewhere else.", I said holding out a hand to calm him down.

"This is your pub as much as their's, you were brought up here with many of these people." he said pushing through the crowd. "and beside there is nowhere else to go the news has already spread around Bristol because of some worthless reporter and his rag of a paper."

The music had started up again to the song Wild Rover and I cast a quick look around the place, catching one or two eye's that turned away from me the moment they realised that I was looking at them. I turned back to the bar just in time for two pints to land on the counter top in front of us. A pair of stools were vacated and I sat down on one, my father sitting on the other.

"What are the police doing about this?" he asked.

"Now I am awake and on my feet, I think that they will probably come looking for me to ask more questions."

"How do you think things will go?"

"I am the only one that truly knows what happened, but I think the police are following their own misguided ideas."

"What about this Professor of yours, the girl's father."

"Isaac, he blames me and will not even look at me, let alone talk to me."

"What will you do now?"

"Tomorrow I will go to the University and see what they say. After that, I will go and see my lawyer and see what he says. As he is both Isaac's lawyer, and mine, hopefully he can act as a middle man."

"Do you have any money?"

"I should do, but will need to check with the bank tomorrow."

"What about work?"

"I don't know, who would employ me?"

My father took a drink from his own pint and sat there looking towards the mirror behind the bar. He was quiet long enough for it to be uncomfortable before he answered. "I haven't got any work going in O'leary's, but I do know that Michael McClay may need help, and he is looking for someone who can deal with paperwork. Why don't you pay him a visit tomorrow."

I looked in the mirror behind the bar, catching glimpses of people glancing towards me. It is work, it is in my blood, and at the moment it looked to be my only option. "I will go around after I've done my errands.", I said finishing off my own pint.

We stayed there for a few more drinks before heading back home. My mother had gone up to bed, but I found a pile of sheets and blankets on one of the chairs. After locking up the house my father went up to bed leaving me to make a bed on the floor.

Chapter VIII
The University, the Lawyer and the Police.

When my father got up the next morning, he found me sat on the floor wrapped up in the sheets and blankets looking at the cold ashes in the fire grate. I don't know if it was the alcohol or the pain from my body protesting about the abuse it had taken, but I hadn't slept at all, I had just sat there.

"Morning son," he said walking into the kitchen and lighting the cooker to boil the kettle. I barely moved and wasn't even sure if I had answered him, I was tired and sat there looking into the ashes hoping for sleep.

"Are you going to see the lawyer and speak to the University Head today?" She asked, as a cup of tea appeared in front of my face and my eyes slowly focused on it, I took the cup in both hands. As my father sat down in the chair next to me, I yawned and nearly dropped my cup as pain from my ribs and arm protested. "Yes, I need to get up and move about or I will be sat here all day."

"You should consider going to see the priest," he offered, "having a chat with him may help you sort how you are feeling now."

I looked at him as if what he had just said was as crazy as what I claimed to have happened that night, but then I just nodded, "I will see what time I have later.", I said and slurped my tea, turning back to look into the fireplace. My mother got up and made us breakfast, and a packed lunch for them both, before they headed off to work leaving me alone. After sitting there until the sun had risen, I got up and got ready to head out. I had to borrow one of my fathers larger shirts, because of the bandage around my arm, along with one of his jackets, but after a wash I looked somewhat more presentable and less like I had just got out of bed. I picked up my bag that contained all my study notes and legal papers that I would need throughout the day and checked that they were all present. Once I was sure I had everything, I picked up the front door key, that my father had left for my use and headed out the door, my bag nestled between my bad arm and chest.

The journey to the University from my parent's house took me up past where Eleanor had been killed, and as much as I wanted to avoid it, I had to visit the place to see if I could remember anything else that had happened that night. I walked all the way across Bristol trying to remember the place where I had grown up and eventually arrived at the restaurant where we had arranged to meet Isaac that fatal night after the show. The area had been cleaned, but there were still patches where blood was faintly visible. As I approached the theatre, I neared the alleyway that was the scene of Eleanor's grisly murder, there was a constable stood by the entrance and as I stopped he looked at me with a combination of boredom and accusation.

"Come to look at the scene of your crime?"

"I didn't ..." I started, but couldn't finish.

"Move along, it will only make you look more guilty." he said glaring at me until I walked away and was out of sight. The University was on top of a hill and I had a bit of a climb to reach it. It took me a while, but eventually I managed to get up the hill, enter the grounds and walk through the front door. After stopping for a few minutes to catch my breath, and waiting for the pain to subside, I climbed up the central staircase that lead to the Headmaster's Office and walked down the corridor stopping outside. I knocked and stood there waiting until the door opened, and his secretary let me in.

"Mr. Purcell, your up and about already?" she asked looking me over, "Did you come to see the Headmaster?"

"Has he got the time to see me?" I enquired.

"I will go and see, I am sure he will want to see you." she said before knocking on his door and vanishing inside. After a while she came back out leaving the door open and waving me inside.

Last time I had been in this office, it had been with Professor Isaac as he begged for me to be admitted into the University to study under him. The room hadn't changed at all from how I remembered it and now I was here begging to be allowed to continue my studies without Professor Isaac's support. We spoke at great lengths about my studies, and the chasm that had opened between the Professor and myself, and what I would need to do to continue my studies. It was explained to me that without Isaac's support, I could not get University Funding and that I would need to find another way to finance the research. I assured him that I was already looking into that and would contact him with these details. After an agreeable outcome, that would allow me to continue studying, I thanked him and left the campus heading toward my next errand of the day.

On my way to the lawyer's office I passed a set of timber framed buildings, which had a courtyard in the middle that held a quiet little café. I needed to stop and get my thoughts straightened out, so decided to stop for a pot of tea and a slice of cake. Despite being hidden down a back alley, the small tearoom was clean and well kept. The outside was painted in a shade of light green and had flowers hanging in baskets above the windows. The little courtyard, that was only accessible from a small stone arch just off the main road, was filled with tables and chairs, but with enough space for even the most generous sized patron to move about. Whatever space was left in the courtyard was filled with many coloured flower pots that brightened up the area, and brought colour to an open area that must only see light for a few hours a day. As I passed under the door frame I looked up to see a sign that had a portcullis and teapot on it with the words "Courtyard Tea Room", I smiled and pushed the door open causing the small bell attached to the door frame to jingle, announcing my entry.

"I will be there in a minute, please feel free to pick a table and take a seat." came a pleasant woman's voice, from behind the counter that was covered in a selection of cakes. I picked a table near the back of the shop affording me a view of the whole room, and courtyard out front as, I waited to be served. I didn't have to wait long for the owner of the voice to appear with a fresh pot of tea.

"Can I get you anything to eat?" she asked.

I looked over to the counter and pointed to a slice of cream and jam filled sponge cake. She nodded at me with a smile, then walked over to pick up a slice and bring it back on a blue painted plate along with a napkin. I poured out a cup of tea and looked to the slice of cake, I felt hungry, but part of me felt sick at the thought of food. After taking a sip of the warm tea, I started to eat. I was almost half way through the slice when the bell rang announcing the entry of yet another patron. I looked up and in the doorway was Mr. Haggit, the lawyer that I was on my way to see. He looked over to me and smiled before winding his way around the tables.

"Ah, Mr. Purcell, I'm glad to see that your out of hospital," he said as he approached my table, "do you mind if I join you?"

"Please, feel free.", I said standing up to shake his proffered hand and wincing before sitting back down.

"Are you sure you should be up and around?"

"No, but would you want to spend many nights in a hospital full of sick people?"

"You have a valid point, people always seem to leave hospital feeling worse." he said with a smile as our host brought him a pot of tea.

"Besides, if I sit around I will start thinking of all the things I could have done that may have saved Eleanor."

"It's too late to think of things like that, from what I hear, if your story about the incident is truthful then there was nothing that you could have done."

He started to look through his pockets and I held up a hand to stop him. "Let me pay for your drink."

"Thank you, but it's not money I'm looking for," he replied absent minded, "I'm looking for my list with the cake orders."

"You wouldn't happen to have one of my trays hiding in your pocket, would you?" our host asked.

He stopped his searching and let his head drop, "I am ever so sorry, dear lady, no I have forgotten it again."

"Find me your list and I will bring the order around myself, and collect the other tray along with the plates that you took.", she said smiling.

Mr. Haggit put his hand in his waistcoat pocket, immediately finding the list, drew it out and handed it over, our host took it and set about preparing the order.

"So what brings you to our little part of the world?" he asked pouring out a cup of tea.

"I was actually on my way around to see you." I replied sipping my own.

The waitress finished getting the order of cakes ready. "Would you mind watching the place for me, Mr. Haggit, while I deliver this lot off and collect my missing items. I will turn the sign over to closed while I'm gone."

"It is in the safest of hands with both of us strong men here.", he said with an over flourished bow, as he walked over to the door and opened it for her. She put her tray down by the door, turned the sign around, then picked up her tray and headed out. Mr. Haggit closed the door and walked back to the table re-taking his seat opposite me. "Would you mind telling me why you want to make use of my services?"

I spent a few minutes taking a drink from my own cup of tea before answering. "Have you heard that Isaac is claiming that I killed her?"

"But you were all so close, you were engaged to be married. What would you have to gain from killing her?" he replied with obvious surprise. He was quite for a while, as he poured out another cup. "Are the police believing him?"

"I do not know, I haven't seen anyone since Isaac threw me out of his home."

Mr. Haggit nearly spat his drink over me, "he threw you out!"

I nodded as I took another drink from my own cup.

"And you agreed?"

"I thought it was best to avoid further trouble."

"Wise idea, he is grieving for the loss of his only child."

The doorbell rang and our host re-entered carrying her trays and missing items. After turning the sign back to open, she carried the items out to the kitchen to be cleaned. She came out a few minutes later to clean up our now cold, empty teapots, and cups. "Well the café is still here, so I thank you gentlemen for minding the place."

"Always a pleasure good lady." Mr. Haggit said getting up. I got up as well, after getting some money out of a pocket and dropping it on the table, I picked up my bag, thanked her and left with Mr. Haggit guiding me to his office.

We walked along the road chatting about how things were standing between Professor Isaac Theologian and I, until we stopped outside a large red bricked building with a castellated roof. The offices of Haggit and Stockwell occupied the third floor of the building and consisted of a collection of rooms spread around one central meeting room with a reception just outside near the stairs. The rooms were all lined with books and ledgers which contained many bound copies of laws and reports on court cases, as well as many other issues, to which their services would come in need off. Mr. Haggit left me in the reception, and after retrieving his slice of cake from the remaining puddings, shuffled me straight into his office, ordering a pot of tea to be brought around. After the tea had arrived and we had consumed our first cup, we got down to business. We continued the discussion about how things sat between Isaac and I, once he had a firm, if somewhat unhappy understanding of the facts, we went on to discuss how I stood with the police and their belief about me being the murderer.

"I won't lie to you, James, I will do what I can to help you, but unless I can get Isaac to come to court and change his mind, it doesn't look good."

"In what way do you mean by, not looking good?"

Mr. Haggit walked around to a cupboard and pulled out a bottle of whisky and two glasses, after filling a glass and handing it to me, he went back to his chair and sat down. He took several deep slow breaths before answering me. "Unless you can find some way to prove what you said is true, you will be arrested for her murder."

My knuckles on the hand that held the glass turned white and I suddenly felt sick. I didn't know what to do or say, I just sat there frozen in place.

Emptying the glass in one swallow he continued, "I am afraid that what I have to say is going to get worse!" Mr. Haggit said from across his desk. With a shaky hand, I raised the amber liquid to my lips and poured it down my throat, there was a warm sensation that followed the liquid down, and when I had lowed the glass, he continued, "I am afraid that if the Hanging Judge is in town, and takes an interest in this case, then you will likely be paying a visit to the executioner."

The glass fell from my hand and shattered as it hit the rug covered wooden floor. "I will be hanged for a crime I didn't commit?" I stammered.

"I hope not, I'd advise you to carry on as if this will not happen, but you need to prepare for the worst case."

Was this the plan all along, was my execution for her death part of some great plan that I was a pawn off, I thought to myself, it couldn't be. My mind was a blur as it went over the events of that night, and the painful memories of what happened after the alley, walking to the restaurant, covered in Eleanor's blood and carrying her body broke through the haze that had obscured the nights events causing me to forget where I was.

"Are you all right, James?" Mr. Haggit asked squeezing my shoulder and breaking me out of the horrible memory.

"I, I, I just remembered carrying Eleanor's body to the restaurant." I stammered in reply. I looked down at my hands in total shock and saw blood covering them and Eleanor's body on the floor in front of me, I felt tears welling up and I closed my eyes to push the tears away. When I opened them again, the blood on my hands and Eleanor's body had vanished. I was going to die and there was nothing I could do about it.

"What are you planning to do now?" Mr Haggit asked

"I don't know, I don't want to tell my parent's about what we've discussed as the shock will likely cause their heart's to fail," I said finally looking up into his face. "I want this kept a secret from them, at least until the newspapers make it public knowledge."

"Have you got any provisions in place, in the event of a worst case scenario?"

"No, I think that is something I need to do." I replied.

Haggit nodded and left the room to find the necessary forms and paperwork, while I sat there lost in thought. After a while he returned and we spent the afternoon working on my Last Will and Testament. Once that was finished I gave him my current address of residence, in case he needed to contact me, before heading out in the direction of my parent's home.

I was thinking about what Mr. Haggit had said when someone shouted, accompanied with the whinnying of a startled horse, I realised that I had walked off the path and into the road. I quickly stepped back onto the path and took several deep breaths before heading home to get some more rest and gather my thoughts.

Chapter IX
Eleanor's Funeral.

It's hard to believe that a week has passed since the attack resulting in Eleanor's death. I was surprised when a few days ago a letter arrived inviting me to Eleanor's funeral from Isaac's manservant. He had explained that Isaac had refused to invite me, but the manservant thought it improper if I didn't come, even if I did not speak to Isaac. Despite not living in the house any more, private mail and letters of condolences still managed to find their way to me. I had made a mental note, reminding me to thank Isaac's manservant for the work he was doing, but I expect he would say that he was just performing his duties.

Up and down the road outside the church a collection of horse drawn, and horseless carriages sat waiting, their owners who were all lining up to give their condolences to Isaac Theologian and say their goodbyes to his daughter Eleanor. I stood by the roofed gate that marked the entrance to the church grounds looking towards the entrance, Isaac stood up by the door talking to friends and colleagues from the University, refusing to even look at me. While many of the same people had talked to me on their way past, none stopped too long afraid of what Isaac may do on this sad day. Many times I had looked up at Isaac, but if he spotted me, he refused to even acknowledge my presence.

"Give it time, Master Purcell." Isaac's manservant said, hiding behind the tall wall that surrounded the church, out of sight of Isaac.

"What has he been like?" I asked, hoping that Isaac hadn't been looking for the monster that had attacked and killed his daughter.

"He is still grieving.", he replied with a look that spoke more then he was willing to say.

"Don't tell me he has been trying to look for it?" I said walking away from the gate to look the manservant in the eyes. He nodded at me, but wouldn't voice what he felt.

"I am sorry for your loss," One of Isaac's friend said walking up to me and taking my hand, "Isaac spoke well of you before she died, he was overjoyed that you two were going to be married."

"Thank you, but I am afraid that is not how he feels now." I said, shaking the offered hand.

"I expect that it has been said far too often, but give him time, he will get over it."

"Thank you," I replied, "I just hope he doesn't go off on his own to find the killer, that's what I am really afraid off."

"Don't worry, we will keep an eye on him for you.", he said, before heading off to join some more friends entering the church.

"How many know what exactly happened that night?" I asked the manservant.

"Only you and Isaac, he said you told him before you passed out."

"What about the people in the restaurant?"

"They don't know anything, apart from Isaac, nobody heard you say a thing."

I looked around the wall, and through the gate up to the church as the last few mourners were entering, Isaac finally looked at me and cast a disapproving glare before turning and entering himself. Once he was out of sight I walked up the path and entered the church, taking a seat on a pew near the door. Under the highly decorated, vaulted ceiling of the church, in front of a cross bearing the crucified form of Jesus stood Eleanor's coffin, as much as I would have like to have looked upon her laid peacefully inside it, I stayed at the back hidden from Isaac's view. Word had already passed around friends and colleagues about our separation, yet I was expected to still attend the funeral. The service was everything Eleanor had once said she wanted her funeral to be, as we had spoken, jokingly about such things one evening, and by the end of the service, there was not a dry eye in the church. When it came to the end of the service the doors at the rear opened and I slipped out before anyone knew I had entered. Running back down and out of the gate I watched as the coffin was carried out and around to the back of the church to where her final resting place was located. I watched everyone leave the church and head around to the graveside, oblivious to me watching them go. When the last group were out of sight, I crept around and watched her burial from behind a wall. In my hands I held a bunch of her favourite flowers, but had to watch and wait until the last of our friends had left with Isaac. Once the site was clear of everyone, but the priest and the grave diggers, I crept out and added my own bunch to the surrounding pile.

"So you showed up then?" came a bitter voice from behind me. I had made sure that the graveyard had been clear before stepping out from my hiding place and was surprised that Isaac had managed to creep up on me.

"Even if you thought not to invite me, I still had to come.", I said standing up and dusting myself down. I turned around to look at Isaac, but he was already walking back to the church, the loose stone and gravel crunching under his feet.

Chapter X
Old Friends and New.

While I could have lived on the money I had in the bank for a while longer, if the case went the way Mr. Haggit, my lawyer, expected it to go, I would need more money. I had heard nothing from, nor spoken to, a detective since the day in the hospital, but from the missives I had received from Mr. Haggit, they were still investigating the murder. In the last week Isaac's manservant had managed to send me more of my bags, my rifle and study notes. I had managed to get more work done on my thesis about the theoretical evolution of dragons, but without biological specimens and the contacts to go looking for some, it would remain incomplete. While my arm and ribs still caused me pain, I was able to work and thought that it was time to start looking for a job. On the night that I had arrived at my parent's house, my father had told me that a job may be available at another boat yard owned by Michael McClay, now I was able to work, and lift things, it was time I followed up on this lead.

Before my father had headed out for work, I had asked him if the job was still going and he had told me that it was, as far as he knew Michael was still in desperate need of help. I left the house and crossed the river leading to the Docklands, but had neglected to ask my father how to find McClays yard. I'm not sure how long I had walked up and down the roads looking, but eventually I came across a large green gate in a wall that lined the whole road as far as the eye could see. Judging from the peeling paint, the gate had not seen much attention for a while and I noticed the white writing was also in a similar state. In one of the doors, I found a smaller door, slightly bigger than me and stepped through into the yard. On the left hand side of the gates, near the door that I had entered through, was a small building with a sliding door that looked to be in the same state as the gates. I looked to the left of the gates towards the warehouse, at the far end was a mallet building with a sign on it "Yard Office," I started walking towards it, but stopped when I heard someone shout.

"What are you doing in my yard?" came a deeply accented Irish voice, I looked around to find its owner and spotted a tired looking red faced man marching towards me.

"I'm looking for work, Sir, my father said that there was talk of you needing help." I replied without thinking. "I was told that you needed someone with good reading and writing skills."

"How good is your reading and writing, are you any good at numbers?"

"I'm a student of the University," I said, reaching into the bag that I had brought with me, inside was my notebook and I pulled it out to show him.

We stood there in the middle of the yard while he read through my book and then stood there a few minutes more while he looked me up and down.

"What about that arm of yours, can you lift and carry?"

"I still have one good arm that can lift and I'm sure I can cope." I responded a bit too defensively.

He signalled to me with a wave of his hand to follow him and he lead me into his office. "Look, I'm under staffed and have several deliveries that need to be sent out by tonight." He said opening the office door and walking inside. There were piles of papers everywhere and I wondered how he managed without help. He threw down the papers he had been carrying and pulled another group off the top of a pile. "If you can sort this lot out by the time I close the gates, you can have a job." He thrust the papers towards me and marched out the door with another pile of papers leaving me standing there feeling bewildered. I followed him out in order to ask him where I should begin, but he had vanished between a stacks of crates and boats that filled his yard. I looked around baffled as to where to start and spotted a worker stepping out from between the stacks.

"Can I help you friend?" he asked with a friendly tone as I approached him.

I held out the papers towards him, "I came here looking for a job and Mr. McClay said I could have one if I could sort out these orders."

"But he didn't tell you where to look for them.", he said smiling. He put down the crate he had been carrying and looked at my papers, he rubbed his chin and looked around the yard. After a few moments, he picked up his crate and lead me over to the warehouse. "Knowing Michael, they could be anywhere, but if there what I expect them to be, they will be in the warehouse near the middle." In front of the warehouses big doors he put his case down and started pulling one side open. As the door opened I spotted dust swirling around in the beams of sunlight and as they opened fully, banging on the bump stops on the outside of the building, I found myself looking up at piles of cases and boxes stacked higher then I was tall. He opened the other door, then after cleaning his hands off, held one out to me. "The names Bobby, for want of a better word, I am the Foreman of this yard."

"James," I replied accepting his proffered hand.

"Are you going to accept the job here if Michael offers you it?"

"It's not like I can afford not to."

"In a bit of money trouble?"

"Not quite."

"Not quite?"

"It's a long painful story that I don't want to talk about." I said looking at him.

He looked at me and noticed the papers I was holding had been screwed up without me knowing. He held up his hands, "fair enough, we all have things we want to keep private." Holding out a hand towards me, he asked, "can I take another look at those orders?"

I handed them over then watched as he flicked though them casting glances down the gaps between the rows. After he handed them back to me he nodded his head for me to follow him down one of the rows. We walked down the length of the warehouse until we reached the middle and Bobby lead me off to an oddly stacked pile of crates and box's on one side. "These came in around the same time as those items on you orders, you should be able to find what you need here," he said looking around, "there should be a trolley around here, somewhere, that you can use to help move things. I hope you find everything you need." I thanked him and watched as he walked back out, picked up his crate, and walked out of sight.

Even with the use of the trolley, it took me all day to find everything and get it stacked into the appropriate pile ready to be shipped out. Every time I managed to get one of the orders sorted, and shipped, there would be another two impatient drivers waiting for me. By the time I had finished, and had watched the last carriage leave, my arm was starting to ache and I was beginning to feel tired. I picked up my bag from where I had left it, closed the warehouse door, and took the completed orders paperwork back to Michael's office. "Sorry I took so long, but the're all dispatched now."

Michael looked up and blinked at me in surprise, "you're still here?"

"You asked me to sort this lot out by tonight and if I did, you would give me a job."

"I didn't think you would stay and get all of them done."

"I don't like leaving a job half finished."

"Any problems?"

"I had to ask one of your men where to look, but once I started to find the first of the items on the orders I was able to locate the others."

"Do you think you can continue doing that while working with others?"

"If you give me the chance, Sir, I will do my best."

He held out his hand, "McClay, Michael Mc-Clay, if you still want the job, it's yours."

"James Purcell" I replied shaking his hand, "what time do I start?"

"I will see you bright and early first thing in the morning."

"Thank you, Sir." I said and left the office. That's one less thing to worry about, I thought to myself, as I headed for the small door in the yards gate. As I exited through the doorway I heard someone call out from behind me. I looked back through and spotted Bobby walking towards me with his own bag over his shoulder.

"Fancy a drink, you can tell me if you got the job or not."

"I should go home and tell my parent's first."

"What about afterwards?"

"Do you mind coming back to my parent's place first?"

"Is it far?"

"Just over the bridge."

"That will be fine," he said with a smile, "the public house isn't far away."

"Let's get going then." I said smiling.

While Bobby waited at the door of my parent's house, I dropped my bag off and told them the news. I told my father I was going out to a pub with the yards Foreman and after a handshake from him, and a hug from my mother, I headed out and followed Bobby to the pub.

"How did it go with them?"

"Their happy that I now have a job and can help them with the bills."

Bobby lead me back across the bridge, then turned right and headed down the road leading away from the docklands. We came to a pub on the riverside and Bobby lead the way inside. I was surprised to see it as packed at this time, but as we pushed through to the bar, Bobby explained to me that it was filled with workers from the surrounding dockyards on their way home. As we stood next to the bar, someone called out my name and I turned around looking for the owner of the voice of the person who had called my name.

"James!" the voice called out a second time and I recognised it as a woman's voice.

"James, what are you doing in a place like this?" came the woman's voice, but this time accompanied with complaints, as a red haired woman pushed her way through the crowds slapping anyone who attempted to grope her bottom.

I watched her push her way through and kick the man next to me off a stool before sitting down on it herself. She was grinning at me and it took a while before the proverbial Galvanic lantern illuminated.

"Shelley?" I asked, bemused.

"Took you long enough!" she said pouting and grinning at the same time.

Bobby looked around realizing that I was talking to someone and interrupted, "you two know each other?"

"Back when we were kids." I replied.

"We used to have a thing together." Shelly answered.

Bobby was smiling at the two of us and I could guess what was passing through his mind. "No, it's not like that!" I said all too defensively.

"Am I supposed to believe that?" He said as his grin grew wider.

Three pints landed on the counter next to us and we each grabbed one. After taking a quick drink Shelly spoke up. "What has it been, five, maybe ten years since we last spoke?"

"Nearly ten years." I replied.

"You have known this trouble maker for over ten years?" Bobby asked looking at Shelly.

"She was the first friend I had when my family moved over here."

"Didn't have much choice, you were about to get killed trying to protect that Chinese girl.", she said pretending to be serious, but failing by grinning. But honestly, back before he left us all behind him, to get his education from the University Professor, we were members of a gang.

"A gang that you used to lead!" I added in, while grinning.

"If it hadn't been for James here, our childhood gangs would still be at war with each other."

"All I did was provide a fight that you could all win by banding together." I added taking another drink. "By the way, what happened to everyone?"

"Some joined the army and navy, some got jobs in the docks, some ended up in the gaol, and as to the others, we just lost contact." she said looking over her pint, "and don't change the subject, you never did answer my question about what are you doing around here?"

"I got thrown out of the Professor's home and had to find a new job."

"So the story is true?" Shelly asked, putting a comforting hand on mine.

"Is this your long story?" Bobby asked.

I nodded, but Shelly interrupted, changing the topic. "Do you have a job?"

"That's why we are here, he got a job working in McClays warehouse and docks."

"Any chance that there could be more work going?" Shelly asked.

"I don't know, you would have to go and ask yourself, why do you ask?"

"I fancy a change from working in this place." she said rubbing her hands together.

"Oh, are you off tonight?" I asked, watching her take another drink

"No, I just decided to take a break when I saw you" she replied with a wink.

"Do you think you can work in a dockyard?" asked Bobby with a laugh

"It can't hurt to try, can it, what time do you start?"

"Seven o'clock." Bobby answered.

"I will be there waiting." grinned Shelly.

I tried to take a drink from my glass and found it empty. I ordered a round of drinks and we moved away from the bar to an empty table and spent the night catching up with Shelly, when she could find

a few moments to reminisce, between serving cus-
tomers .

Chapter XI
A New Start.

The next morning I was woken up by my father, as he made his way into the kitchen, "celebrating last night?" he asked noticing that I was a bit hungover.

I pushed myself into a sitting position and groaned as my arm protested about the added pressure on it. "Sorry if I woke you last night."

"I take it that you met a few people you previously knew?"

"Bumped into Shelly last night and was catching up on what I have been missing."

"Is she keeping out of trouble?"

I got to my feet and put my bedding into the cupboard under the stairs. "She's working in the pub we went to, but is looking for a new job."

My father walked into the kitchen, lit the stove and put the kettle on to boil. I still hadn't told him what Mr. Haggit had said to me and I hoped that now I was working, we could all forget about the ongoing investigation. it wasn't long before my mother joined us in the kitchen, where she proceeded to push us out, as she started making breakfast. I sat down on a chair and father handed me a cup of tea he had managed to make before being kicked out.

"When do you start?"

"This morning.", I said, taking the cup and taking a drink. Mother put three bowls of porridge on the table and we joined her for breakfast. After Father and I had finished, we got ready for work, while Mother prepared our lunches, and once we were all ready, we headed out. We crossed the bridge to the dock area and said our goodbyes as we headed off in our separate directions. Mother's route took her north towards the hospital, while my father and I headed towards the docks, separating halfway down the road.

When I arrived at McClays gate I found Bobby stood there waiting for me. "You made it then?" he said putting an arm around my shoulder.

"Only just.", I said checking my pocket watch and following Bobby through the gate.

I walked over to the yard office, knocked on the door and waited to be called in. When Michael called out, I entered and took a seat on the other side of his desk and waited for him to finish what he was writing. "I didn't think you would come back."

"Why is that, Sir?"

"You just don't seem like the kind that would work here."

"Things have changed in my life and events have caused me to fall back to what my family has always done for a living."

Michael put down his pen and leaned before he continued "I'm going to come straight to the point. I am a good judge of character, but from what I have found out about you, I would say that your life has been interesting."

I looked at him and felt nervous, I was not quite sure what to say, but I was sure of what he was talking about. I looked him in the eyes, and though I felt like shrinking away, I told myself that I had to keep eye contact. He looked down to his desk and pulled out a newspaper that had a story circled in red pencil. "This says that your fiancée was killed when you were both attacked leaving the theatre. It also goes on to say that the police suspect you of her murder."

My eyes fell to the floor and I felt ashamed of what had happened that night. I remembered that he was still looking at me, and forced myself to looked back up.

"I will only ask this once, if you can answer it while looking me in the eye, then I will accept your answer, did you kill her?"

I took a deep breath, never breaking eye contact and replied, "I did not kill her, I loved her and we were about to be married."

He sat there studying me for a few uncomfortable minutes before he spoke. "Yesterday you showed me evidence that you could read and write and said that you were a student of the University. I spoke to a friend of mine who says you have a high reading and writing standard, I need help with record-keeping, as well as making sure that deliveries and collections are correct. Do you still want the job?"

"Yes, Sir, very much."

"Good, welcome to the yard.", he said as he reached over his desk to shake my hand. With the deal done and the job now mine, he picked up a stack of ledgers and handed them over to me. "My warehouse is a mess and in desperate need of sorting out. There is an office in the warehouse, somewhere, when you're not sorting out collections and deliveries I need you to sort through these records and rearrange everything in there, so that the records all add up and are easy to track." He reached down to a pile of paper on the floor, flicked through them then handed some to me, "these orders also need to be sent out today, can I leave them in your hands?"

"I will make them top priority for today, Sir." I replied.

As if on command, Bobby appeared at the door.

"Mr. McClay," he started, "oh, James you still here."

"What is it Bobby?"

"There is a Miss Lee outside, we were talking about James starting work here and she asked if there was any more work going."

"Do you know this lady, James?" Michael asked looking at me.

I nodded, "from a long time ago, but I didn't think she would seriously come here when we spoke last night."

"Bobby, take James into the warehouse and help him find the stairs to the old office. I will speak to Miss Lee and decide if she wants to work here or not." Bobby nodded and I lead the way out with my arm full of ledgers and papers. As we left the outer office door I said a quick hello to Shelly before Bobby told her to go in. The warehouse hadn't been opened up yet and we had to use the small door in the front. I set my bundle down on the first crate I came across then helped Bobby open up the main warehouse doors, allowing the early morning sun light to flood into the dark warehouse. Bobby lead the way through to the back doors to open them, and while they didn't provide as much light, they allowed us to locate the office and begin the search for the stairway that lead to the office's door. We had to move several stacks of crates during the search, but eventually we found the stairs, and after retrieving my pile of paperwork from where I had left it I headed up to the office to make myself a place to work.

"Where do you want to start, cleaning the office or making a start on the orders?" asked Bobby.

"I told Michael that I would sort the orders out first. Once we have them ready, I will know how much time I have spare to clean this place.", I said putting the paperwork down, sending up a plume of dust.

"Where do I start looking for this lot?" I asked Bobby picking up the first order sheet from the pile.

After a coughing fit Bobby managed to catch his breath and answer, "this first lot should be near the roadside wall of the warehouse," he said, "this second lot on the order sheet should be near the back close to a boat waiting for repair. This final lot, I am afraid is somewhere in here.", he said waving towards the dirty and dust covered windows.

I split the rest of the orders into two pile and gave one set to Bobby, "you take this lot, I'll take this lot, and we will stack them near the entrance."

"Sound like a plan to me, just don't go getting lost in here.", he said with an amused look as we headed out of the office and down the stairs. When we reached the bottom we found Shelly waiting for us.

"How did it go with Michael?"

"He doesn't seem convinced, but he is willing to give me a try." Shelly replied looking around.

I looked at Bobby who nodded back to me, "there is an office up there, if you dump your bag, then come back, Bobby will show you where to get started." With a smile she ran up the stairs, returning quickly. Bobby laid out his pile and started explaining to Shelly where to start her search.

Bobby and Shelly walked off in one direction and I went off in the other, grabbing the first hand cart I could find. I followed the wall to where Bobby said the first batch were to be found and after a bit of a search, I found them under a canvas, beneath a bricked up window. I loaded them up onto my trolley, thankful that they were not heavy, and deposited them just inside the warehouse doors. Once I had them all organised, I took the first piece of paper and put it on my dusty desk under a lump of iron. The second set provided more elusive and just as I was about to give up and move to the next set I came across them under a massive canvas. The canvas covered an area nearly the size of the warehouse and as I looked under it I found a great grey hull of an airship, with the missing crates hidden under it. I made a mental note to come back when I had the time to check out the ship, but for now I had crates to shift. By the time I got the second load back to the warehouse doors and unloaded from the hand cart, Bobby and Shelly were returning with another load.

"How is the search going?" Bobby asked.

"These ones proved a bit hard to find.", I said as I heaved one of the cases off the trolley.

"But you found them, then."

"Yep, hiding under the airship."

Bobby looked at me and scratched his chin in thought. "My God, I had forgotten that was still here."

"Does that happen often?" Shelly asked.

"What, forgetting where stuff is stored?" Bobby looked to be deep in thought, but then he chuckled, "Yep, it is why Michael needs your help with the paperwork."

"What's the ship's story?" I asked.

"It was brought in years ago while the owner arranged for repair, but a few years back I heard he got a new ship and left this one to gather dust."

"Do you know if it's up for sale?"

Bobby's eyes went wide, "Do you think you may be able to afford it?" he almost shouted.

"No, I'm just curious."

"You will need to speak to Michael about it.", Bobby said rubbing his chin.

"You want me to add these to the pile in the office?" Shelly asked pointing to the papers for the two loads we had just brought around.

"Thanks Shelly.", I said and handed them over to her, before heading off back into the yard. By midday we had found the orders that Bobby had thought were hiding in the yard and had started on the stuff hiding in the warehouse.

Midway through the afternoon the first of the carriages turned up to collect the loads. Bobby and Shelly ran off to find the rest of the orders while I began to load up.

"Excuse me mate, you Mr. Purcell?" a voice said from behind me. I turned around and found myself looking into the chest of a giant of a man. "Sorry mate.", he said taking a step back and I looked up into a pair of bright and friendly eyes.

"I am James Purcell.", I said holding out my hand.

His big hand wrapped around mine. "Call me Mr. Ibbs, Mr. McClay says that you need some help."

"Thank you Mr. Ibbs, if you can help me load this lot up, maybe we can get the rest ready for dispatch a lot faster."

He grinned at me. "Say what needs to go where and I will get it done."

I explained to Mr. Ibbs what needed to go on each cart and by the time I had finished loading up the current cart, he was just finishing his second. The weight of the crates didn't seem to bother him and he loaded them as if there were empty, leaving me to sort out the forms.

In only a short time, the five carts that had been waiting were heading out the gate, making room ready for the next batch of carriages to arrive. I picked up the papers and was just about to head up to my office, while Mr. Ibbs took a drink from the bottle he took from a bag he had set near the door, when Mr Ibbs asked me a question.

"What would you like me to help you with next?" he asked watching me.

"I haven't got anything else until I sort out the next batch, do you know Bobby?"

"Yeh, worked with him a few times."

"Good, can you help him while I dump this into the office, please?"

"Sure, but where is he?" Mr. Ibbs asked.

I looked down the central walk way and could not see anyone. "Bobby, Shelly" I shouted out.

"Down here near the back." Bobby called out and Shelly's head appeared around the side of a row of cases. Mr. Ibbs handed me the papers he had, then headed of into the warehouse to join Bobby and Shelly.

I headed up to my office to deposit the current collection of completed orders, and perhaps finally make a start on sorting out the ledgers that Michael had given to me. After a while of looking through figures and lists, I leaned back and rubbed my eyes, I heard the stairs creaking as someone walked up them and a few moments later Bobby came in grinning.

"Did I just catch you sleeping on the job?"

I pulled my watch out of my pocket and popped open the case. "Just rubbing my eyes, how on earth can you find anything in here with these books like this?" I closed the watch cover after reading the time and popped it back into my pocket and stood up.

"We just keep looking until we find what we need!" he said, "are you ready to stop for lunch?"

"I am feeling a bit hungry." I replied reaching down to grabbing my bag from under my desk before heading down to join the others

With Master Ibbs help, we were able to sort out the rest of the days work, allowing Bobby to go back to being the yards Foreman, and getting the dockside workers back under control. In the following days, we settled into our now normal working lives and slowly I managed to put my troubles to the back of my mind and start making a new life for myself.

Chapter XII
Doctor Montgomery Silver.

He heard a carriage pull up outside his surgery followed by the carriage door being opened and closed, and his building's front door being opened and closed. He had a backlog of paperwork that he was trying to catch up on and didn't hear the footsteps of someone climbing the buildings stairs. When the door to his rooms opened, jingling the little brass bell that hung above it, he put down his pen and walked out to the reception, come waiting room.

"How may I help you, Miss?" he asked looking at a woman dressed in an orange, almost red, dress with silver trim.

"I am in need of you assistance with a little problem I have."

"And what kind of problem would that be that would bring a lady like you to my humble establishment?"

"Is there somewhere more private where we can discuss this?

"I assure you madam, my treatment room is the best place to discuss things in private."

"The problem is not really mine, but with a friend. It just happens that it will affect everyone around him and he is not in the position to sort this out by himself."

Doctor Silver looked at her to see if he could find a clue to what she was alluding to, but realising that her posture would give nothing away he held out a hand and guided her into the treatment room, locked the door, then guided her into his private study that was hidden beyond. He indicated that she should take a seat in front of his desk, then after shutting and locking the door he offered her a drink that she politely refused. After pouring one for himself, he sat down on the other side of the desk and watched as she pulled a pin out of her hat, before removing it, to allow her long red hair to fall down around her shoulders and back. He watched her run her fingers through her hair to straighten it out and marvelled at the silver streak that ran from her forehead down it's full shining length

"If I may ask, and I assume that is the reason that you came to speak with me, what is this problem that your friend has that prevents him from seeing a doctor is person?"

She looked up into his eyes and he realised that they were of oriental shape and filled with both sadness and a touch of anger. "Doctor Silver, do you remember clearly the events in the restaurant?"

"The injured boy that came in covered in blood and carrying his poor dead fiancee, yes, I remember that clearly."

"And what of the wound to her?"

"The savage wound that looked like it was caused by a wild animal?"

She nodded at him before continuing. "I hear tell that the police are saying it was caused by a man holding a weapon."

"I know, they have been trying to discredit my statements in the tribunal by claiming my observations a fallacy and that their own police surgeon claims them to be man-made."

"Are you willing to stand up in court and state that they were made by an animal?

"As I have said, many times already, yes, I am willing to stand witness. Why do you ask?"

"I believe that your life may be at risk by those who are trying to discredit you."

"To what end, and why are you getting involved. Surely your own people will not want to risk having anything that will endanger their treaties with the British Empire involved."

"There is no connection to my people, as you put it, the boy, James Purcell is an old childhood friend and I believe there is something going on that requires him being found guilty of murder."

Doctor Silver rubbed his eyes and took another drink. "I suspected as much.", he said causing her to look startled.

"Are you aware of something going on?"

He reached into the top draw of his desk and pulled out a revolver, "Yes, I am aware, but I do not know what your connection to this is."

The lady held up her hands in submission, "I am not the enemy here. I want my friend to be free and safe and I believe that you can help me save him."

"And what would you have me do?"

"Have you made provisions incase you are prevented from attending the trial?"

He nodded to her, "I have a written statement given to two separate law firms to be handed to the attending judge incase I can't make it. Do you expect me to give you their names?"

"Absolutely not," she replied shaking her head, "but incase anything happens to them, would you mind letting me have a copy, as an extra precaution, should anything happen to prevent you from giving evidence?"

"And how can I trust that you would hand over the letter in the event of the other two copy's going missing?"

"I give you my word as the daughter of the Emperor of Japan's most trusted Samurai."

"How can I tell that you are not making this up?"

"What would you have me do, kneel before you and beg?" she asked standing up and walking around to stand beside him, adjusting her dress, she then knelt down on the floor in front of him, lowering her head to the floor. "Please, Sir, I beg of you, give me a copy of your statement and help save my friend."

"Madam, please!" Doctor Silver responded in shock, "there is no need to prostrate yourself in front of me in such a manner." he said, putting down the gun and holding out a hand to help her up. "You have shamed me, so much so, that I will do as you asked, just to make up for you having to beg in such a way."

She accepted his hand as he helped her to her feet and he could see that tears had marked her features disturbing her makeup. Pulling a handkerchief from his pocket, and guiding her back out to the privacy of the treatment room so that she could clean up the water marks from her face, he went over to a draw that he kept locked in his study, pulled a key from around his neck, and with a flick, opened the draw and pulled out an envelope that contained another copy of his statement. She came back into the room a few moments later and when he offered her a drink, she accepted, swallowing the drink in one swift move that made her cheeks glow as the amber fluid made its way through her system. A smile grew across her delicate features as he held out the letter.

"Madam, I apologise for my behaviour, and I hope that you have not damaged you own honour due to my actions."

She wrapped his hand in her own, "Just promise me that you will do everything in your power to help my friend and all will be forgiven."

He knelt down on the floor in front of her, and still holding her hands replied, "You have my very word on this, I swear on my own life, and upon my pledge as a surgeon." He stood up and pushed the letter into her hands then guided her around the desk to where her hat rested.

She replaced the hat on her head, but didn't pin up her hair. Thank you, Doctor, that is all that I can ask.

Do you have a carriage waiting for you, if so, may I escort down to it?"

She nodded letting him lead her out of his rooms, down to the front door, where he helped her up into the carriage, before watching it disappear into the foggy night.

Walking back through the front door, he checked his pocket watch and found the time to be later than he expected. He closed and bolted the front door then went up to his rooms to fetch his coat, hat and bag. When he got up to the reception area he found a man waiting for him, he had no memory of passing or seeing anyone in the stairwell, yet here was another visitor. "I am sorry, Sir, it's getting late and I need to go home.

"Oh, my apologies for the lateness of my visit, but I promise that this won't take long."

"And what business would you have with me at this late hour?"

"The animal that killed that girl, would you like to know what it is?" the man said, as he continued looking around the doctors collection of African souvenirs.

"Can we do this tomorrow, as I am afraid that I really do have to leave."

The man looked away from the wall hanging and towards the doctor. "As I said, this won't take long."

The strangers smile made a cold sweat appear on the doctor's forehead and he suddenly remembered the words that the lady in red had said. He tried to run into his study to get his pistol, but heard a ripping sound before a powerful hand grabbed his arm. He was turned around and came face-to-face with a snarling monster that towered over him.

"Wh, wh, what are you?"

"I am a Lycanthrope."

"What do you want with me?"

"I am afraid that the boy must be found guilty and executed for the murder of the girl."

"But there is no way that he could have done it."

"Maybe, maybe not, but I am afraid that you will not live long enough to give your statement to the court."

Doctor Silver didn't get a chance to make any sound, other than a gurgle, as one of the creatures claws flashed out and ripped open his throat and major arteries in his neck. Blood decorated the walls, along with the memorabilia from his days in Africa as the monster watched the life drain from the man. When he was sure the doctor was dead he left the rooms, headed out through the back door, and walked off into the fog.

"Is the Doctor out of the way?" said a voice from the shadow.

"Ah, Detective Brass, how nice to see that you have arrived to investigate such a grisly murder. I hope I haven't made too much of a mess for you to sort out."

"I am honoured that you regard me with so much esteem that you would speak with me."

The beast walked over to where the detective waited and stood over him. "Just remember the deal, if you keep to your part of the plan, then you will get what you want."

"I just need to find a reason to arrest the boy now."

"Do not worry about that, we have a plan ready."

"Well then," Detective Brass said doffing his hat, "we will speak again in a few days when I have the boy as a guest in my station." He watched the creature disappear into the night, and after waiting a few minutes, blew on his whistle that would alert any constable in the area to the fact that a crime had been committed.

Chapter XIII
Confrontation with Isaac.

For the last few weeks I had fallen into an easy pace of working life and had managed to put my worries to the back of my mind. My little group had grown by two more men and our team had made good steady progress with our work. Bobby had gone back to working as the sites Foreman, ordering the other crews around, leaving me to look after my own team. After a full and satisfying days work we had made our usual pilgrimage to the pub before heading towards our individual homes. Shorty after I had arrived back at my parent's house, a messenger came knocking on the front door. He was stood there holding up a hand in which he held a hastily written message from Isaac's manservant. The message stated that Isaac had located a werewolf in Bristol and had headed off after it to hunt and kill it. I stepped past the messenger and was about to close the door when I realised that he was still stood on the doorstep. "Is there something else?" I asked and watched as he fidgeted on the spot.

"I need an answer to the following question I am to ask, to take back with me, will you go and stop him?"

"Do you know the contents of the letter?" I sharply asked

"The letter?" he replied confused, "no, but the manservant asked me to ask you for an answer to that question."

I folded up the letter and told the messenger that I would see to it. He waited on the doorstep bouncing on his toes, it took me a moment to realise that he was waiting for a tip for his service. After handing him an amount that raised a smile on his face, he darted of to deliver my response.

"Who was it?" my father called out.

"A messenger. I have to go out, Isaac is in Bristol looking for the beast that killed Eleanor!"

"Don't do anything stupid," he warned, "we don't know if you're still being investigated for Eleanor's murder."

"I have to do this, I can't let Isaac go after this monster, he'll just get himself killed." I said as I lifted my long coat from it's hook and pulled it over my still bandaged arm.

"Are you going to take your rifle?" he said walking over to the cupboard were it resided.

"No, if anything happens and I'm seen with it, then it will make my standing look even worse."

"Take care, I have already lost one son, I don't want to lose another."

I stopped walking towards the door and turned back towards him, this is the first time that Robert, my brother who was never spoken about, had been mentioned in any pervious conversation I had had with my father, except that one time I was told that I had an older brother, and even then, all I was told was that he left home before I was born. Any questions I had about Robert would never get answered and I was told to leave the matter be, which I did, but now questions about Robert resurfaced filing my thoughts, blocking out my mission, but my father had turned his back on me and I knew I would get no answers to those questions yet again. I turned back to the door and opened it. "Do not worry, I will be back tonight.", I said as I walked out the door closing it behind me.

As I made my way across the docks and up into Bristol to where Eleanor was attacked, I concentrated on my mission to find Isaac. I thought of the hundreds of questions I needed to ask him, I thought about were the conversation would lead, and what the end results could be. I imagined all the various directions in which the conversation could lead and was grateful that I hadn't brought my rifle. I crossed the city centre and made my way up the road that lead to the theatre, and the scene of our attack. To avoid being spotted, I headed down a back road and approached the alley from the rear.

"Have you come to watch as I kill the old man?" a voice asked from behind me. I turned around to come face-to- face with the beast that had caused me so much heartache and trouble.

"I have come to stop him from getting killed." I said

"I wouldn't worry about him being killed, we still need him alive to guide your actions.", said the beast, smiling at me.

A gun shot rang out and I felt a sting in my arm where something, a bullet maybe, grazed it. "So you are, connected to that creature, I was right to blame you for Eleanor's death!" Isaac cried out from the far end of the alley.

I spun around to face him and heard the creature walk away behind me. "Isaac please, I did not know the creature was going to be here." I pleaded.

"But you knew I was?"

"I received a message that you had come to Bristol in search of the beast and I thought you might start from here to look for it. I had to come and stop you!" I took a step towards him and noticed that the rifle had not been lowered. I held up my hands with palms facing him and took another step. "Isaac, please, lower the rifle."

"Tell me why I should lower it and not save the police the pleasure of hanging you."

"Isaac, you are a good man, not a murderer."

"Unlike you?"

"Isaac, I keep telling you that I didn't do it!"

"Yet I watched you talking to the creature that you claimed kill her."

"Isaac surely you must have seen the wound, it should have been obvious, that even the most dimwitted person, could tell that it wasn't caused by me."

Isaac slowly pulled the rifle lever down loading another bullet into the chamber. As if time had painfully slowed, he raised the rifle so that it was pointed between my eyes. "All I have been told is that the wound severed a major blood vessel in her shoulder and that her death was rapid." His already age wrinkled face contorted with anger, I feared for Isaac's life and soul, more than my own, and knew that I had to act. With speed that even surprised myself I grabbed the rifle and pulled it out of Isaac grasp. I cranked the load leaver rapidly to empty the rifle then handed it back to him.

"Isaac, go home, people need you, don't waste your remaining life tracking down this monster."

For several uncomfortable moments we stood there watching each other, I noticed his shoulders start to shake before he collapsed to the cobbles that lined the alley. "Without Eleanor, I have nothing to live for."

I knelt down next to him placing the rifle on the ground. "Isaac, you are the most prominent expert in Mythobiology, you have researched more creatures than anyone in the world, without your work at the University these creatures would remain as just stories."

"Who else is there that needs me?"

"What about your cook and manservant, without you, they would have no job and no money to pay for their home, plus they love you." He looked at me with the expression of someone unsure of what had happened. I stood up and help him to his feet before hailing a carriage to take him home. "Isaac, let me deal with the Lycanthrope, concentrate on your work and your friends, they are there for you and will be glad if you would go and see them." I could see that he didn't trust me, but he allowed me to guide him into the carriage that had stopped beside us. I gave the driver a generous tip and ordered him not to stop until they arrived at Isaac's home and to make sure he walked him to his door, where he would be greeted by the staff waiting for him there. With a nod, the driver pulled away and headed off down the hill, away from the theatre. My pockets were filled with the unused rifle bullets I had taken out of Isaac's gun, then remembering that I had left it in the alley, I went back to pick it up before heading home.

As I opened the door to my parent's' home, I had a feeling that I should look back down the street. I followed this feeling, but all I saw was a quiet, empty road, so why did I get the sickening feeling that something was wrong and that I had made a fatal mistake.

The carriage made its way along the streets and roads leading out into the countryside, the driver smiled to himself, the boy had no idea what he had done, nor that he had sealed, not only the old man's fate, but also his own. As the carriage entered a wooded road, it stopped and two other gentleman climbed in. It carried on into the woods , were fog surrounded it, but it never came out of the other end of the road.

Chapter XIV
The Arrest of James Purcell.

In the morning, bleary-eyed from lack of sleep, I stumbled in to work and up to my office in the roof of the storage shed. I had not been there for an hour before Shelly came running up the stairs, almost falling through the office door. With a hand on both sides of the door frame Shelly struggled for breath.

"What is the matter Shelly, what's wrong?"

"Michael just sent me to come and get you, you need to come down to his office immediately!" she said between great gulps of breath.

"Do you know why?"

Shelly took a few more deep breaths before continuing. "No, but there is a Black Maria in the yard and police are swarming all over the place."

I had been expecting this day for so long, but now that it had come, I was at a loss about what I was going to do after so many weeks of no contact with the police, since the day I woke up in hospital after the murder of Eleanor

"James, what's going on?"

"I am in need of your assistance Shelly, I need you to sneak out of the yard and take a message to someone for me as quickly as you can."

"You know that I will do anything for you, what do you need me to do?" she said with a scared look on her face.

I reached into to pocket of my jacket and pulled out a small slip of paper. "Go to Haggit and Stockwell, the solicitors, and tell them that you need to get a message to Mr. Haggit."

"What message do you need me to deliver?"

"The worst case day has come!" I said slowly."After that I need you look after my parent's, I don't want them to know what is going on for as long as possible."

"Of course, but why?"

"If today ends up the way I expect, then my freedom is at an end."

"And you think that me being there will stop them finding out?"

"No, but your presence will be appreciated when they do find out."

A look of confusion mixed with fear crossed Shelly's face. Looking like she was about to collapse to the floor, I stood up from my chair and guided her into it before her legs gave out. Once she was seated, I put a reassuring hand on her shoulder and she forced a smile to curve her lips. "They have come to arrest you for your fiancée's murder, haven't they?" she asked, I nodded. She grasped one of my hands, "shouldn't it me me reassuring you?"

"If this was a surprise to me, then maybe. I have been expecting this day since Eleanor's murder. I was advised to carry on and live in the hope that this day will not come."

"You went and found a job knowing that you could be arrested for her murder?" Shelly asked and I turned around to grab my jacket.

"We hoped that the police would find enough evidence to prove my claim of innocence, but with circumstances being the way they were that night, there was only a slim chance of me remaining a free man."

"And you lived these last few months with that small hope?"

I smiled and nodded, pulling my jacket on adjusting it so that I looked as presentable as possible. I reached over to the desk and picked up my site keys and placed them into Shelly's hands. "Looks like I will be leaving things in your capable hands."

"You think Michael will keep me on and give me your job if you get arrested?" she asked looking down at the keys. I watched a tear fall from her eyes and land on the rusty surface of one key.

"Do you think you would still be working here if Michael didn't trust you?" I asked as she fought to gain control of her feelings. When the shudders subsided, she took a deep breath, stood up and placed the keys in her pocket. "Ready to go and confront the inevitable?" I asked. She nodded and together we headed down the stairs, out of the warehouse and across the yard to the door that lead to Michael's office. As Shelly had said, a distinctive black carriage stood in the middle of the yard and workers had started gathering to see what was happening. Bobby appeared between a stack of crates and walked over to me.

"Do you know what is going on here, James?"

"It's been a pleasure working with you Bobby." I replied trying to keep a smile on my face. "Can you do me a favour and look after Shelly and my little team?"

"Yes, but why?"

I looked at Shelly and nodded, with a silent goodbye, she turned around, walked towards the gate and left the yard. Bobby watched her leave before turning back to me, "where is she going?"

"Shelly's running a message to my lawyer, can you cover for her?"

"Why."

"Please Bobby?" I pleaded, my voice sounding pathetic.

Bobby looked at me and then I watched as he realised what was going on. "Is this to do with ...." he started, but stopped himself from finishing the sentence.

"That carriage has come for me and it looks like my time working here may be at an end." I replied looking towards the door to Michael's office.

"I know it's been only a short time we've been working together, but sure, I will cover for her and help your team."

"Thanks Bobby." I took a deep breath and opened the outer door. Once it was closed, I knocked on the inner door and waited until I was called in. After adjusting my appearance again, I walked through the inner door and into Michael's office for possibly the last time. As I entered I spotted Michael looking out of his window along with two Detectives, with a constable waiting for me.

Michael waited until I closed the door before he turned around and faced me dead in the eye. "If you remember when you came to me, I asked you to look me in the eye and tell me truthfully if you murdered the girl, will you look me in the eye now and swear your innocence again?"

I kept my gaze locked on him as I answered his question, "I swear on my own life, the life of my parent's and the life of Shelly Lee that I did not kill Eleanor Theologian, my fiancée!"

He looked at me, our gaze's never parting, eye's never blinking, as if he was searching deep in my soul for the truth. After what felt like an eternity, he finally nodded and spoke. "Despite what these Detectives say, I believe you. Even though you have only worked for me for a short time, I want you to know that if there is anything I can do to help, please let me know."

"Thank you, but you have enough to worry about running your own business, but may I make one last request from you, would you do me a favour and give Shelly the chance to show what she can do to prove her worth to you."

"I can do that, but rest assured that she has already proved herself to me and my boys. Do you have a lawyer?"

"I do and he has already been sent for."

"Well then, I wish you the best of luck and hope that you can quickly sort things out and return to us."

"Thank you Mr. McClay I said before turning to the Detective's. Brass stepped forward, "Do you know the whereabouts of Isaac Theologian?"

"No, why?"

"Last night you were spotted in an alleyway talking to him, a witness says that he watched you help Mr. Theologian into a carriage and then pay the driver."

"Is there something wrong with paying a carriage driver?"

"No, but Mr. Theologian has not been seen since."

"Do you think that I paid the driver to kill him?"

He pulled out a pair of handcuffs, "James Purcell, I am arresting you for the murder of Eleanor Theologian and the disappearance of her father, Isaac Theologian. Will you come along quietly?"

I held out my arms and he fastened the handcuffs around my wrists. I turned back to Michael, and with a bow, thanked him one more time before being lead out of the office and into the waiting carriage. With the aid of a constable, who held my good arm in a vice like grip, I climbed up to and sat on one of the carriage's benches. As I looked out the back of the carriage door I could see that the crowd had mixed looks of shock or sadness at my predicament, and was glad that my parent's were not here to witness this. A few of the constables came back to the carriage and climbed in with the Detectives before the door was shut and the carriage lurched forward as the two black horse's put their weight into taking the carriage and its passengers to its next destination. As we travelled I thought about how rough the ride was and how the carriage that had brought me back to Bristol had been more comfortable and stable. It was quite a surprised that with the possibility that my life will soon to be over, without a miracle, all I could think about was the rocking ride in this rickety thing. After a while the carriage came to a stop and I was lead out of the back and into the police station courtyard to find Mr. Haggit and Shelly waiting. I stood and waited while Mr. Haggit talked to the Detectives.

"James, are you going to be ok?" Shelly asked while Haggit explained his purpose for being here.

"I don't know, but you have a job to do, Michael and Bobby will be relying you to take over my duties."

"I don't know if I can."

I grabbed her hands with mine still in cuffs, "You are Shelly Lee, who was once one of the leaders of one of the biggest gangs of kids. You fought off those people who tried to take away Lou Way, you handled that and I am more than sure you can handle the job in Michaels yard." I could see her eye's watering and full of doubt, but she straightened up, wiped her eyes with her sleeve and forced a smile.

"Take care James.", she said and left the station.

I turned back to the Detectives to find Haggit arguing with Brass, while Cobble and the constables stood back watching the confrontation. After a while Haggit's shoulder slumped and he took a step back. Detective Brass came over to me, grabbed me by the arm and lead me into the station and into one of the cells. Haggit followed us and waited until after I was put in a cell, the handcuffs removed, and the cell door locked. I stood there watching as the constables left followed by the Detectives and the door to the cell block was closed. We waited a few more minutes in silence to make sure that we were on our own, then opening my jacket and waist coat,

I sat down on a bench and leaned back against the bars. I took a deep breath and turned towards Mr. Haggit.

"Isaac is missing as well now?" I said

"So I heard, from Shelly, please tell me if you know anything about this, James."

"I hadn't seen or spoken to him since the funeral and even that was only a terse, one-sided conversation. I have, however, been in contact with his manservant."

"By what means is this contact?" Haggit asked.

"We have been using a messenger to send letters back and forth. I have kept all my correspondence and so should he.", I said looking around at my abysmal surroundings.

"Do you know where Professor Isaac Theologian is, James?"

"He should be at home"

"What do you mean by, should be at home?"

I took a deep breath looking towards the door to give me time to collect my thoughts. "I have seen him since the funeral.", I said with a sigh.

"What do you mean?"

I pulled a letter from my waist coat pocket and handed it over. Once he finished reading it he looked up, his eyes bulging like saucers. "Did you see him last night?"

"Yes, and he shot me in the arm."

"Why did he do that?"

"Eleanor's killer was in the alley waiting for me, Isaac spotted me talking to him and got the wrong idea."

"What happened afterwards?"

"The creature fled, and Isaac thought to shoot me again."

"What did you do then?"

"I persuaded Isaac to give me his rifle, before I put him in a carriage and sent him home."

"Going by what the Detectives have told me, he didn't arrive home, do you know where he could have gone?"

"No, I have no idea, I paid the driver extra to make sure that he would be taken straight to his home and assisted to the door, without stopping."

"Can you describe the driver or the carriage?"

"No, it looked like every other horse drawn carriage in Bristol, and the driver looked the same as all the others. All I can say was that he was parked just up from the restaurant, near the alley."

"Do you think he could have told the driver to change direction and go somewhere else?"

"If he has, then I expect that he has gone after the creature, despite me trying my best to stop him last night by sending him home.", I said looking up to the ceiling of the cell. I was going to die because no one would believe me if I told them the real reason of Eleanor's death. "How have you been proceeding with setting up my defence?"

"The police are holding their case notes closed so all I have to go on is your statement and the doctor who was at the restaurant when you walked in." Mr. Haggit replied.

"No one else?"

"No one is willing to talk, it is as if someone has been telling them to keep quiet."

"What can you tell me about the witness interviews?"

"The first one was held in the restaurant the day after the attack, I only found out about it after you came to see me, from what I have seen, and heard from the other witnesses, it would seem that the police are rewording the witness statements to make sure that you are judged as guilty."

"What do you mean?"

"In the last inquest, it was established that Eleanor died from the wound to her shoulder, but they mentioned nothing about the fact that it was caused by an animal, and the fact that there was no weapon, that could cause such an injury, was found anywhere in the area."

"So what are they using to prove my guilt?" I asked dismayed, while trying not to raise my voice.

"All the witness that were in the area, and in the restaurant, stated that they saw you, and only you enter the alley and restaurant with Eleanor."

"What about photos of the scene and the street?"

"What was there to take pictures off, you know all too well that it was raining heavily that night, most of the blood was washed away, and you removed Eleanor from the alley and brought her to the restaurant." Haggit replied fiddling with the catch on his bag. "I am surprised that you didn't know any off this?"

"I was never asked to attend any off the inquiries, in fact until now, I have not seen nor heard from a single detective or constable since the day I left hospital." I said looking towards the door. "What do I do now, what will happen to me?"

"Well one good thing, you will not have that much time to wait for a trial as they waited until now to arrest you."

"When is the trial?"

"The day after tomorrow."

"That soon?"

Mr. Haggit nodded at me before continuing. "I was hoping to have this matter resolved by now, our company is doing everything we can to end this but we are preparing for the worst case."

"Any chance of an appeal?"

"I don't believe so, but we are also working on that as well.", he said and stood up. "I am sorry, James, but I have to return to my office to prepare for your trial. Don't give up."

I stood up and held my hand out to him through the cell's bars, he took it, gave it a slow shake and I thanked him before watching him head out of the cell area.

I didn't get to sit there long without company. After the amount of time it would have taken Mr. Haggit to get back to his office, the cell block door opened and Detective Brass entered, without his shadow, Detective Cobbler.

"Are you ready to answer some question without the presence of Mr Haggit?"

"What can I tell you that you don't already know?"

"Why not give up this fantasy about being a victim and confess to murdering both Eleanor and Isaac Theologian."

"I will not change what I say to something that is not true!

"Are you absolutely confident in that?"

"Why?" I asked watching as a smile crossed Brass's face.

"I'm sure you know how this looks, you were seen entering a dark alley after Eleanor Theologian, there was an exchange of angry words heard coming from it and then you exciting the place a few minutes later carrying her body and covered in blood."

My jaw worked in frustration as I struggled to think of a response. I wished I could think of something that didn't sound crazy, but my failure was proving to be an amusement for the Detective.

"What about her father Isaac Theologian, do you know where is he?" he asked

"As I said back in Michael's office, I put him in a carriage and paid the driver to take him home. If he didn't get home, I have no idea where he went. Why don't you go out and find the driver?"

"Well, let us hope that for your sake we can find a driver that can confirm what you say." he said studying me. He turned away and started heading to the door, as he got to the door he stopped and turned back. "Oh one more thing before I go, where is the rifle that you were seen carrying across Bristol?"

"Back at my parent's house, why?"

Detective Brass didn't answer, but smiled as he left the cell block leaving me to my own thoughts and fears.

Detective Brass picked up his coat from the hanger in his office and left the station. Walking across town, he weaved his way through back alleys to a more questionable area and walked into one of the many drinking establishments. Taking a seat at the bar, he ordered a drink and looked at his reflection in the mirror behind the bar, as another person sat down beside him.

"Is it done Detective?"

"He is in custody at my station."

"And you can guarantee that he will be found guilty?"

"I'm sure that your activities over these past few weeks will lead others to the correct decision."

"We need him to be hanged."

"I'm sure that with the evidence we have against him, along with the correct amount of persuasion, the Judge and Jury will work in our favour."

"Everything depends on his execution, the deal will not be completed until he is dead."

"It is as good as done." Detective Brass said, then swallowed the last of his drink and left the bar.

Chapter XV
The Trial of James Purcell.

I didn't see much of Detective Brass yesterday until the afternoon, and even that was brief. He was smiling when he entered the cell block and asked the same questions as he did when he arrested me. Even though he didn't push me in an effort to get me to confess to the murder of Eleanor, I felt like there was something else going on. Today was the start of my trial and from what I understood, all the preliminary evidence and statements had already been given to the attending Judge. I was handcuffed and lead out of the cell to a waiting Black Maria with a group of constables and the younger Detective Cobbler. The strange absence of Detective Brass, put me on edge and as I was helped up into the back of the carriage, the feeling of uncertainty as to the outcome weighed heavy on my mind. Once the constables and Cobbler got themselves seated, the door was closed and the carriage rocked into motion on it's journey across Bristol to the courthouse. As the carriage turned the last corner into the road leading to the courthouse, the drivers brought the carriage to a halt.

"Why have we stopped?" shouted Cobbler from the cabin.

I felt the carriage rock as the driver climbed down and a moment later the door open."The road ahead is closed by a large crowed. What do you want me to do, push through or go around?"

"You had better go around, we need him to actually reach the courthouse and be found guilty before he is executed." The Detective said looking towards the crowd.

"Yes, Detective." the driver said before closing the door. The carriage rocked again as the driver climbed back up onto his seat and turned the carriage around to head down one of the side roads.

The carriage wobbled as it turned and I managed to see a huge crowd of spectators who looked like they had come to see my trial. I was glad to see that none of them had seen us, as the sound of their heckles and shouts drowned out the sound of the horse and carriage on the cobbled road. After a few moments, the carriage came to a halt again and rocked as the driver climbed down from the seat. There were more revellers waiting for us, but the constables who had ridden with me were more than capable of dealing with them. The carriage door was opened and the constables climbed out. After some shouting I heard a gate opening and the carriage started moving again. The journey wasn't long and I watched as we passed under a foreboding arch that spanned the entrance to the rear of the courthouse. The carriage came to a halt, and after some more shouting, the constables passed through the gate and it was locked up behind them. The door to the carriage was opened and I climbed out to find myself stood in the middle of a yard at the back of the courthouse. After a brief exchange of half heard words between the Detective and the courthouses guards, I was lead through a door leading to a collection of prison cells in the buildings basement. After being escorted to a cell, I was locked in and I listened to another exchange of words before the footsteps of the Detective and guards faded away down a corridor.

I wasn't alone for long before Mr. Haggit arrived. "How are you holding up James?"

"As well as can be expected for a person who will probably be declared guilty of murder. What of my defence?"

He blinked and I spotted dark lines around his eyes, a sure sign of lack of sleep. "I am sorry, from what I can tell, it is as I feared, there are far too many witness statements putting you in a bad light and the evidence they have gathered leads to you as the killer." I looked over to the door of the cell block and was silent long enough to make the atmosphere uncomfortable. "There was a small chance that we can save you." Mr. Haggit offered, and I turned to him and noticed he too was looking at the door.

"Was?"

Mr. Haggit leaned back against the wall, directly across from my cell and looked even more stressed, "there has been a change to the charges drawn up against you."

"What kind of change?"

"Professor Isaac Theologian has now been missing for three nights. I have been informed that Detective Brass went around to your parent's home and found a rifle belonging to the Professor."

I cursed, I should have made sure that it had been sent back to the house, but I had completely forgotten about it until after my arrest.

"James," Mr. Haggit started, "it has been fired and the prosecution has petitioned the judge to include the murder of Isaac based solely on the rifle and his disappearance."

"Of course it would show traces of being fired, Isaac shot me with it!"

"Why would he do that?"

"The murderer turned up in the alley and Isaac, in his grief, believed that I was working with the killer."

Mr. Haggit was quiet and I could see his mind working feverishly as he thought about how to proceed. He didn't have long to think about it, the cell door creaked open on old rusty hinges to reveal two constables standing waiting. "Come along now, time for your trial." one stated in a deep mid Irish accent. Mr. Haggit and I stood up to made our way over to the cell door, but as we approached, the constable held up a hand and stopped us. I looked at him then held up my hands and pulled them apart making the little chain between them jingle. He looked down at them and smiled before moving forward to open the cell door and pointing the way out towards the courtrooms.

As we walked along halls and climbed up stairs, I could hear the ever-growing noise of people talking in both fearful and excited tones. While some were excited and wanted to get in to hear the evidence and make up their own minds, others had already decided that I was guilty. I could make out each one of them passing their own judgement and arguing over what punishment I should receive for my crimes. We walked along a corridor approaching the ever-increasing voices then turned away and entered a doorway that opened into a small corridor lined with wooden benches. At the end of the corridor was another door, which I was lead through and into the courtroom.

As I entered the sound in the room stopped and I felt all eyes turn towards me. Mr. Haggit was guided to a table and behind him I spotted Shelly and Bobby watching me with sorrow in their eyes. As I was lead to a small box in the middle of the room I looked towards them and smiled, watching as they attempted to smiled back. I climbed up into the box and looked around the court at all the people who had come to watch me on trial for my beloved Eleanor's murder, and now also for her fathers. On the highest balcony, next to a door I noticed three men sitting with a gap separating them from the closest spectators as if those around were afraid to get close to them. All three of them were watching me with obvious interest, but I had a feeling that they were here for other reasons. One of the three was a young gentleman, but the other two, who were older, held themselves as if he was in charge. In the middle sat a gentleman with grey, almost white hair who was chatting to a middle aged, largely built man, sat next to him. The large man stopped talking and looked towards me, and I got a feeling that we knew each other, he scowled at me then went back to whatever his conversation had been. I looked back to the youngest of the three and noticed that he was studying me as if trying to work out what I would do. I turned away and started looking at the others around the galleries and recognised various people I had met over the years, including some of the people that had been in the theatre on that fateful night. On one end of the spectators benches sat a lady dressed in red and silver who was chatting to a much older gentleman. As I looked at her, her head tilted back slightly, and from below her hat, her exotic eyes locked onto mine. I felt like I knew her from somewhere.

A door in front of me opened and as the Judge walked out the noise in the room, from people talking, increased with excitement and it took quite a bit of shouting to silence the court. The Judge sat down and when the court had remained quite long enough, he looked over to the Prosecutor and held up a hand to signal that he should start outlining the case that had been brought against me. For two long hours, as the Prosecutor talked, I had to sit and be quiet as he described a murder, that I had supposedly planned out, telling lies that caused me to flinch, and earning me a stern looks from the Judge. Several times there were hisses and murmurs from the spectators, so that by the time he finished his opening statement it was almost lunchtime. When the Prosecutor had sat back down, the Court Clerk stood up and addressed the court. His speech was brief, his only purpose here was to present the chargers that the police had brought against me. Once he had finished, he sat down and the judge looked up from his notes and looked straight at me. I looked back at him and looked into his eyes, he made me feel nervous, but I had to make sure that I didn't look away.

"James Purcell, you have been brought here to stand trial for the murder of Eleanor Theologian, and the disappearance and suspected murder of her father, Isaac Theologian. Do you understand the serious nature of the charges brought against you this day?"

"Yes I do, your Honour." I replied back looking into his eyes.

"And how do plead?"

"My plea on this day is not guilty!"

"To which charge do you plead not guilty?"

"To all of these charges." I replied. I heard several voices around the room as people discussed what I had just said as if they had been expecting me to plead guilty.

The judge called a recess to the proceedings for lunch and I was escorted back-down to my cell. During the break I was soon visited by Shelly and Bobby.

"That has to be all rubbish, the Prosecution is doing everything he can, including lying, to make you look guilty!" Shelly said shaking with obvious anger while Bobby kept a hand on her shoulder, "He's made it all up."

"What can I do, I have to wait until he's finished before Mr. Haggit can present my case." I said in reply.

Bobby pulled out a sheet from a newspaper and handed it over to me, "I had hoped to keep this away from Shelly, and your parent's, but I doubt that I have been successful."

I took the paper from him and began reading. It was impossible not to understand what was in the paper as the main heading read "The Trial of James Purcell, Murderer of Eleanor Theologian begins to-day!"

"What is the word about the docks?" I asked.

"I have never known most of the workers to even read the paper, but the talk is mixed. Some support you, some are against you. We have avoided anyone fighting, but we think there may be some violence before this is all over."

"What of Mr. McClay?"

"Master Ibbs is watching everything going on while we are away."

"Has there been any problems with reporters, or nosey visitors?"

"The gates are closed and only open to allow in those with business dealings, deliveries or collections."

I nodded and handed the paper back to Bobby and watched as he guided Shelly out of the cell, a comforting arm around her shoulder. A scant few minutes after they had left I was joined by a constable who had come to guide me back through the building and up to the courtroom.

Once everyone had returned to the courtroom and the court had been silenced, the Prosecutor stood up and I noticed a smug grin on his face. "This isn't the first time that you have killed someone is it Mr. Purcell?"

I was about to answer, but for some reason looked up to the red lady, who while casting me a sidling glance, was chatting to her companion. I looked over to Shelly and watched her eyes go wide before she covered her face and looked away.

"Ah, I see that Miss Lee remembers this event, will one of you like to explain to the court what had happened?"

Shelly removed her hands from her face, but refused to answer, I looked back to the lady in red, whose eyes were so full of sadness, and suddenly had a flash of recognition. If this lady was the girl from back then or just looked like a grown-up version of her I didn't know. I looked back at Shelly and mouthed "Sou Young!" Shelly flashed a looked towards the lady in red then quickly towards the floor.

"I must remind you that you are in a court of law, please tell us what happened that day."

I took a deep breath and in a voice that sounded almost like the Prosecutors, I began "due to the nature of the events that day, no one involved in that event will talk out because they were are all sworn to secrecy." The truth is that the events of that changed all of us. Some of us changed for the better and some for the worse. The day had resulted in a boat owner and his daughter being rescued, but resulted in the deaths of five men and one of our friends.

"What is the meaning of this, why won't you tell the court what happened that day?" bellowed the Judge.

There was a cough from the balcony and the eyes of everyone in the court turned to look at the man sat with the lady in red.

"Lord Judge, may I address the court?"

"Do you know the accused?"

"No Lord Judge, I am just here as a spectator and assistant to my fellow Trade Ambassador who wished to learn how our courts work."

The Judge looked over his glasses at the man and held his hand up allowing the Ambassador to address the court.

"As a Trade Ambassador for the British Empire I am aware of the event to which the Prosecutor is talking about. Unfortunately, due to current trade negotiations I hereby officially petition the court to cease this line of questioning and delete any reference to it."

"And under what ground should we consider such a petition?"

"Let me just say that if the event came to light, our position on the table of negotiations will be harmed and you will lose both your job and your estate."

"Are you threatening me to save the life of this man?" The Judge asked pointing to me.

"No Lord Judge, I took valuable time out of trade negotiations to accompany my companion here as a spectator. I'm glad I did otherwise a terrible mistake could have been made."

The Judge looked at him trying to decide what to do, after a few moments he indicated that the Ambassador should sit down before addressing the court. "I accept your petition, and will abide by it.

Mr. Prosecutor, you also heard the request and I order you to comply with it."

"Yes Judge." came the Prosecutors reply and I watched as he sorted out his papers and put a collection in his bag.

Temporarily stalled in his accusations, it took him a while to rearrange his thoughts. The Prosecutor started by describing the cause of Eleanor's death and it took me a few moments to work out that something was incorrect about what he was saying. I had been informed that a doctor who had been in the restaurant when I carried her body in had described the wound as caused by a wild animal, but here, in this courtroom, the prosecutor was reading out a report from a different doctor. Mr. Haggit argued this and called for the weapon that had caused it, but the Prosecutor claimed that I had disposed of it in a method that prevented the police from ever finding it.

The Police Doctor, who was supposed to have examined and recorded Eleanor's cause of death was called to stand and Mr. Haggit argued every part of his report. Mr. Haggit had told me about the other doctor who had been in the restaurant and had examined both Eleanor and myself at the time. When the Police Doctor had finished, the Judge turned to him.

"Mr. Haggit, you claim that another doctor who was there at the restaurant, claims the cause of death to be different, is he here today?"

"No Judge, he promised to be here, but he is mysteriously absent."

"Has he been called to give witness?"

"Yes, Sir!"

The Judge was quiet for a moment as he looked down at his notes. After a while he looked up. "Mr. Haggit, what is the name of this doctor?"

"Doctor Montgomery Silver, Sir."

I watched as a constable stood up, approached the Judge and whispered in his ear. After a few moments, the Judge looked around the court then towards Mr. Haggit. "I have just been informed that the Doctor, in question, was found dead in his surgery. Did he leave any kind of statement?"

"Yes your honour, he feared that something may happen to him and left a signed, written statement with my company."

"Objection, your honour," the Prosecutor shouted, "How can we guarantee that this written statement is genuine?"

The Judge looked from Mr. Haggit to the Prosecutor and back to Mr. Haggit, eventually he waved a hand to bring the letter forward. He put on a pair of gold rimed spectacles and started reading, once he had finished, he looked up to me then back to Mr. Haggit, "the Prosecutor makes a valid point Mr. Haggit, how can you prove that this letter is genuine?"

"My Lord the letter that you have is signed and counter signed by a witness as is required by the law. The letter was handled by a colleague of the company acting as a lawyer for the Doctor."

"Yes, but how can your company prove it, did he write the letter in front of your companies partners?"

There was another cough from the stands and the lady in red summoned the Courts Bailiff. After a short exchange, the Bailiff passed the message to the judge who looked up towards her. "Is this true, you also have a copy that was given to you by Doctor Silver?"

I watched as the lady opened her purse and pulled out an envelope that looked exactly like the one that Mr. Haggit handed to the Judge. He compared the two in front of the whole court, ripped them up eliciting shock from everyone in attendance. "I am sorry to say this, but the Prosecutor's objection stands and I cannot accept these. Unless you can find another way to prove your Doctors claims, then I find I must go with the finding of the Police Surgeon." After a long pause while Mr. Haggit stumbled to find another means to discredit the Police Surgeons findings. The Judge spoke up. "Are we finished examining the medical examiner?" the Judge asked and when both Mr. Haggit and the Prosecutor nodded the doctor was dismissed.

After that, other evidence was discussed and the first day ended with a heated argument between Mr. Haggit and the Prosecutor until the Judge was forced to call a halt to it. He pulled out his watch and looked at the time. The time was late and the case was suspended for the next day with everyone dismissed. I expected to be taken back to the police station, but I was guided back down to the cell in the court, where I was given an evening meal and left there until the following morning.

After what passed for breakfast, the trial continued with statements from the many witness that had been in the theatre, the restaurant and the road that night. The theatre had been packed along with the restaurant and it took nearly two days to get through them all. After what Mr. Haggit had said, if this trial was to be decided on just   the witness statements, then I was in serious trouble. All of the witness statements from the street said that I was seen walking into the alley with Eleanor then coming out a few minutes later covered in blood, carrying her body. Such was the amount of identical statements that I was starting to lose hope. When all the witness statements had been examined and cross-examined, it was time to call on those who could defend my innocence. Shelly was called forward to give her statement, but before she could start, the Prosecutor started to object.

"Objection, Shelly Lee is a known gang leader and is to be considered a hostile witness. It is the belief of the Prosecution that she will likely lie to protect James Purcell!"

"No, you can't do this" Shelly shouted out. I looked around to see Bobby trying to get her to sit down.

"Silence Miss Lee," the Judge shouted, as he hammered his gavel against his bench to hush the many shouting voices.

"Your Honour, you cannot allow this." Bobby called out.

"And who are you to be making suggestions on what the court can and cannot do."

"I am James Purcell's Supervisor, both Miss Lee and I have been sent here in Mr. Michael McClay's, James employers, stead."

"Well then, if you want to be heard in this court, shut up, sit down and wait your turn to be called forward." the Judge shouted, banging on his desk. "I am aware of Miss Lee's record as well as their earlier connection. She is to come forward and give her statement!"

Shelly described how and why we first met, how I came to be a member of her gang and that I had stopped the infighting between the gangs. She then went on to describe the events that led up to our going separate ways, then how we met and started working together for Michael McClay. The Prosecution argued with everything she said, and even tried to insinuate that she may have been involved, but Mr. Haggit had already checked up to confirm that she had been working in a pub on both nights in question, and had many witnesses who could testify to the fact. When Shelly had finished, Bobby was called forward, and even though I had only known Bobby since starting the job, he described how reliable an employee I had been for the company since. When Bobby was finished being accused of various things by the Prosecutor and released to return to his seat, a few more people were called forward to testify to my innocence. There should have been more people including the University's Professors, but when they had found out that Isaac had disappeared, they had all refused to come. With no one left to call to give defending or prosecuting statements, the fourth day came to an end. The last day of the trial started with a summing up of all that had been discussed and a repeat of the charges that had been raised against me.

"Now that the evidence and statements concerning the murder of Eleanor Theologian have been given," the Judge started, "the Prosecution will bring forwards its evidence for the disappearance, and possible murder, of the girl's father, Professor Isaac Theologian."

The Prosecutor stood up and waved a bailiff forward who was carrying something wrapped up in brown paper. "There has been no sign of the Professor since the night before the trial. This," he pointed to the item, "has been identified as a rifle belonging to the missing Professor and shows the tell tale marks of having been fired on the night of his disappearance."

"What do you have to say about this weapon, James Purcell?"

"As I told Detective Brass, I came across Isaac in the alley way and he fired it a me. I took the rifle from him and persuaded him to give up the foolish hunt."

"Then what happened?"

"I put him in a carriage, giving the driver a generous tip to make sure that Isaac was taken home."

"That's strange," the Prosecutor started, "According to the Detectives none of the drivers, who were working that night, went anywhere near that alley and have no memory of ever speaking to you, or having picked up such a known Professor."

"There has to be, I am not making this up, I put him in a carriage and watched it drive away."

"I propose that you indeed put the Professor in the carriage, knowing that he would accuse you of his daughter's murder, paid the driver to dispose of the Professor and go into hiding."

"No, that's not what happened."

"With no one to stand witness to what you claim, is there any way that you can prove your innocence?" the Judge asked. I hung my head in shame, "no your Honour!"

"Then as the presiding Judge, without evidence to prove you didn't commit his murder and no sign of the Professor to prove your innocence, then I must approve of the Prosecutors charge." He turned to the jury, "You have seen and heard all the evidence in this trial for the murder of Eleanor Theologians, and the disappearance, and suspected murder of her father, Professor Isaac Theologian, I will now dismiss you to make your decision."

The Jury was dismissed to discuss their verdicts, but from their whispers throughout the trail it didn't look good, The newspapers I had been shown had made me out to be a murderer and with the number of people reading them it looked like the Jury wouldn't take long to agree with what had been printed. As suspected, due to the newspapers, the public had been turned against me, and after fifteen minutes the Jury returned.

The Judge looked up from his own notes and turned to the Jury, "I take it that you have come to a decision?"

"Yes, your Honour, all the members of this appointed Jury agree to the decision." replied the elected Jury Foreman

The Judge turned to me before letting the Foreman continue. "Before this court passes judgement on you, James Purcell, do you have any last words to say?"

I stood up, looked at the Jury then spoke "I did not kill my fiancée Eleanor Theologian and I have nothing to do with Isaac Theologian's disappearance." I said

The Judge turned back to the Jury. "You have heard all the evidence and heard all of the statements given by witnesses. What is your verdict?"

"Guilty!"

"To which charge?"

"Both. The Murder of Eleanor Theologian and the suspected murder of her father Isaac Theologian." The appointed Head Juror said. With these words, the court room erupted with the noise of the spectators shouting their agreements.

It took the Judge several minutes to quiet the crowd through shouting, threats and the constant banging of his gavel, but in the end the court room fell silent so that the Judge could speak.

"James Purcell, by due process, you have been given a chance to defend yourself against all charges brought against you. It is the decision of the court and of the Jury presiding over your case that you have been found guilty of the grisly murder of Eleanor Theologian and the suspected murder of her father, Professor Isaac Theologian. Under Common Law, on this day, you will be taken from this court and imprisoned in the New Gaol to live your remaining days until your sentence in carried out. In one week hence, you will be taken from your cell to the gallows where you will be executed by hanging. Your body will be left hanging for a minimum of one hour until the prison surgeon can pronounce you to be officially dead . Your body will be afterwards buried within the precincts of the prison, in which you shall be confined after your conviction, may the Lord have mercy upon your soul" the Judge pronounced.

My knees buckled under me and I collapsed to the floor, I had hoped that the court would be persuaded to see sense through due process, but that was not to be. The spectators started shouting at me. Mr. Haggit spoke to me as I was hoisted to my feet by a pair of constable. "James, I am sorry, we have tried everything we could."

"What do I do now?"

"We are already working on an appeal and resting our hopes on that, but I must beg of you not to do anything hasty. Do what the warders say and don't cause any trouble," he replied. As I was pulled from the room, I looked up to the three men, who had spent the whole time in the same seats throughout the trial, to see them smiling with dark looks as if they had planned all this.

I was taken through the building and out into the courtyard I had first arrived in, and climbed up into the Black Maria carriage that was waiting to take me to the New Goal. The carriage rocked back and forth as it travelled and only stopped after it had entered the gaol's courtyard. A pair of warders guided me into the main building and I said good-bye to the world outside.

Chapter XVI
The Execution of James Purcell.

The swirl of fog that always preceded their entry into this world was hidden by the fog that was already present. The three had come to witness the end of the first step in their long plan concerning the boy, and they were here to make sure it happened the way it needed to happen. As they stepped out of the thicker bank of fog trapped between two buildings they were joined by several more men. Like the youngest of the three, the additional men were dressed in the uniform of the Camalonian guards, their sole purpose here was to storm the prison and make sure that their leader was unhindered in his access to the boy before he swung from the rope. None of them spoke as they made their way to the prison, they didn't need to, everything that could possibly happen had been accounted for and all they needed to do was follow their orders. They made their way towards the prisons entrance, but stopped a street away. The youngest of the soldiers would wait to make his move just before the boy was to hang. The old gentleman and his companion walked on and joined the crowd that had gathered outside the gate.

Hidden from view on the roof top above the soldiers, another person knelt watching these events unfold. She was not supposed to be present, her

time to be with James had not yet come, but ever since he had saved her as child, she had kept a secret vigil over him. Her keen Kitsune senses had alerted her to the presence of the werewolves below, and even though they were her enemies, she was forbidden to interfere with their plans. The destiny of the Kitsune and the Lycanthropes depended on the dark one's taking the first steps, and she could only hope that the elders were correct that their intervention in twenty years time would save his soul from the coming darkness. She would have liked to get closer to watch the execution, but that would result in her presence being known to others. Knelt here on the roof, she would have to content herself with watching the events through her other senses.

Six days and seven nights I have been here. Six long days followed by seven even longer nights, have I sat here in this prison cell. When you know that your life is about to end, time seems to slow down to a crawl, minutes stretch into hours, hours turn into days and days, well, they feel like a whole lifetime. I haven't slept very well since they passed the guilty judgement on me, guilty of a crime I didn't commit, in a trial that was twisted against me.

Even Mr. Haggit felt the trial had been set against me from the beginning, but there was nothing any of us could do about it. My mind was switching through emotions faster than I could count, one minute, I felt remorse and regret, the next I was feeling anger and hatred, but now I was feeling sick. So sick that I had refused my finial meal for fear of decorating the cell walls with it.

I hadn't been completely alone for the whole time. They had allowed me some visitors, both Shelly and Bobby had called by to help pass the time, but these visits had been few and far between. Mr. Haggit had also visited, to keep me updated on the appeal they were trying to raise, but with today being the scheduled date of my execution, time and hope had run out. On the second day I had been visited by the artisan warder who would be assembling and adjusting the scaffold for my hanging, I also had a visit from the undertaker who measured me up for my coffin, but I hadn't been left alone when these visitors left. Several times I had been pulled from my cell and made to join the other prisoners in what the warders called "compulsory yard exercises", exercises which were nothing more than walking in a circle around the yard for hours on end.

As if on cue the door to my cell opened and in walked the prisons Chaplin, who stepped to one side of the door and started to read from his Bible. The executioner and artisan warder walked in carrying several strong leather straps and pinioned my arms to my sides and my wrists together behind my back. I took a deep breath as I looked out the door to see the Governor of the gaol stood against the far wall with the Under Sheriff on one side, the Deputy Governor and Prison Surgeon standing solemnly on

his other, with a group of additional warders flanking them on both sides. As the executioner and warder went about their work, the Chaplin stood next to me muttering about God having mercy on my soul, but all I can think of as I stand here being bound up, is that I hope God's wrath is unleashed against the Lycanthrope that had destroyed my life. I don't know if it was at this point that I started to realise how much I wanted to live, but I knew then, that I wanted to get revenge against the people who had done this to me. I started asking whatever deity existed to help me live and survive this. When the preparations were finished I was guided out of the cell and along the block to the corridor that lead out to the yard to where the scaffold waited for its next short term resident.

The young officer leading his soldiers looked up to the clear patch of sky around the prison, then down at the face of the pocket watch in his hand. With a smile, he closed his watch and ordered his men to move forward. Unlike the soldiers he was leading, he wasn't a werewolf but could still sense the presence of the Kitsune above them. "I hope you're not here to interfere with the events today?" he asked over a mind link he forced on the watcher.

"That is not my purpose on this day, black soul."
She spat back over the link. "If things are to follow
the destiny foretold by the ancients, then no matter
how much I detest things, I must wait for you to
make the first move."

"I am honoured that your kind will not interfere,
Princess." came the reply, the charm and sarcasm
easily detectable over the link. Closing his mental
link to the watcher and approaching the prisons
door, he banged hard. "Let me in this instance, if
you do not comply, you will be responsible for the
murder of an innocent man." When no reply came,
the young man whispered a spell that blew the door
open. His men charged through, knocking over any
man who tried to stop them and destroying any door
closed in their path.

As I waited in front of the last door that lead
outside, I began to feel scared that this truly was the
end. I felt regret for the things I had not done and
my mind raced through all the what-ifs, as if it was
trying to find a way out of this one way trip. They
were not the only emotions that ran through my
mind, I was feeling angry and frustrated that I
couldn't help myself, and sorrow for my parent's
whose honour had been lost through their son being
found guilty and executed for murder. The door
opened and warm sunlight crept through the opening filling me with warmth as more of the light

reached me. When the door had fully opened I was lead out to the yard with my party, the prisoners who were exercising stopped as we approached, parting to allow us through. As we advanced up to the gallows all, but the executioner and the warder holding me, lined up on the ground to watch as I was lead up the stairs and placed on the spot marked on the trap door I would fall through. More straps were added to my ankles and around my knees and I was thankful because without them my knees would be shaking so much they would be bruised from knocking together. A white cloth bag was placed over my head and I felt the hang man's noose place around my neck and pulled tight. I listened to the footsteps of the executioner walking over to the leaver that would open the platform below me ending my life. Suddenly, I heard several booms from deep inside the prison and a commotion from the direction of the door that I was lead from. I heard the door burst open and what sounded like several men running into the yard.

"Let me through, you must stop this at once, the man that you are about to kill is innocent!" a voice was shouting across the yard.

There was a shuffle of feet on the platform, someone swore, and I felt the platform disappear from beneath me as I fell to my death followed by a sharp pain in my neck as my falling was brought to a halt. The rope jerked tight, forcing my wind pipe closed and I found myself unable to breathe. The ribs and bones in my arms that were still healing from the attack broke again and my mind was flooded with pain. I had promised myself that I wouldn't fight it, that I would let death come naturally, but something was wrong. My internal warning alarm that had proved so helpful during my studies, was going off. I had been told that the process of hanging would be quick and that the weight of my own body would snap my neck, but here I was still alive, flapping around like a fish on a line, gradually suffocating as the rope slowly tightened from my body weight pulling it down. I was starting to see stars from the lack of air into my lungs and I felt my consciousness closing in around me, the last thing I remembered before my world turned black was thinking, "So this is what dying feels like."

Chapter XVII
Is this Death Eleanor, my Love?

Darkness surrounded me but I did not panic or feel fear, for a moment I was at peace, but for a whispered word that was floating around me. I stood there in the darkness listening to it, something in it sounded familiar and I felt a sadness in my chest and tears welling up in my eyes. Someone was calling to me and with a great force of will I opened my eyes to find myself in the middle of a band-stand. For a moment I was confused, the last I knew, I was in a prison hanging on a rope, but now, here I was stood against the handrail of a bandstand looking out over a park filled with bright flowers. I looked up to the clear blue summer sky and felt the sun's warmth on my face. For a moment, everything was forgotten, all that mattered was the here and now. I felt hands wrap around my waist and I turned away from the sun. Letting out a heavy sigh, I looked into the familiar hazel eyes of Eleanor and my hands found their way around her waist and I smiled.

"Am I dead, Eleanor my love, are we to be to-gether again?"

She said nothing, but slipped from my embrace, gabbing my hand in one of her's as she lead me over to a table that had been setup in the middle of the bandstand where another person seat with their back to me

"Isaac?" I asked, tentatively fearing what he would say, and watched as he stood up and turned towards us.

This man was not Isaac. As he stood and turned towards me I could see he was around the same age and height as Isaac. His hair was silver and matched the silver gray of his suit and waistcoat. In one hand he held a cane and as I studied it, I noticed that the hand grip was shaped to resemble a miniature human skull. His face was warm due to his smile and he gave me the feeling that he had shared a joke with Eleanor a moment before she had interrupted my looking into the sky.

He put a hand into a pocket and pulled out a card handing it to me. "I am afraid not, but for the sake of this meeting, you may call me Mr Death."

"Your not how the stories describe you." I blurted out without thinking.

"We have tried hard to shed that image." he said with a nod. "Would you care to sit and take tea with us?" he asked pointing to a chair.

"Yes he will, good Sir." Eleanor said leading me around the table to the two other seats waiting there.

We sat down and Eleanor poured out the tea for all. I picked up the cup and sniffed the perfume coming from it momentarily forgetting the world around me again. I looked through the drifts of steam towards the old man and remembered the question that I originally asked Eleanor. "If I am not dead, then where am I?"

"That is a hard question to answer, this garden can be thought of as purgatory, the place between heaven and hell. In truth, it is a spirit realm that allows the spirits to communicate with the living."

"What you see around you, James, is a recreation of one of our shared memories. I was chosen to act on their behalf to help you to adjust and get back to your life." Eleanor said as she sipped from her own cup.

"But why am I here?"

The old man plucked a watch from his waistcoat and checked the time, "It would seem that we are running out of time and need to get straight to the point. Something is going on which is disturbing the balance, whatever it is, it is giving you a second chance of life. Whomever is behind this, you must not trust." he said, as a bobbin of string appeared in the air. "This represents your lifeline, as you can see, it is long and very knotted. Your life is going to be very hard but you need to keep going and trust in your instincts."

Turning to Eleanor I asked the question burning in my mind. "Will we ever be together again, Eleanor, my love?"

She gave me a sad smile and I instantly felt her loss. "No, I am afraid that by the time you next come by this way, I will have long moved on." She leaned over and kissed me, "Goodbye, James my love, let those around you help you and remember that no matter what happens, your friends will always be there for you."

I was about to say something, but out of the corner of my eye I noticed that the colour was disappearing around us. We stood up and as I watched the world faded to gray, then to black before I felt something pulling me away.

"Do you think that by dying, you would be free of our influence?"

51511810R00084

Made in the USA
Charleston, SC
23 January 2016